Thirty Centuries
of Solitude
and Then?

Fernand W. Dahan

Bethesda Communications Group

Published by the Bethesda Communications Group
4816 Montgomery Lane
Bethesda, MD 20814
www.bcgpub.com

ISBN-13: 978-1-7321501-2-6
ISBN-10: 1-7321501-2-5

Drawings on pages 16, 20, and 21 are by the author. The drawing on page 23 is by Samir Zoghby.

All proceeds from the sale of this book will be donated to The Knights Children Of Hope, a charitable organization that serves children with special needs.

In memory of my wife, Anita Dahan,
and Dr. Marcel (Magdi) K.,
and in honor of Dr. K's granddaughter, Kendall D.

Contents

Acknowledgments

I wish to thank Samir M. Zoghby and Roberta Culver for their assistance in editing text, and Roberta Culver for her assistance with the dialogue. Also, thank you to Paul Levine for helping proof the book and to Deborah Lange for editing text, placing images, and formatting the book for publication.

Preface

About ten years ago, I was in Philadelphia, Pennsylvania, at the wake of a well-known aesthetic surgeon, who happened to be a cousin of mine, as well as a very good friend. I sat at the table of his daughter and her husband, as well as their daughter. I knew his daughter when she was six months old; then, separated by the distance, we never had the opportunity to see each other again till her father's funeral and his wake. During our conversation, we caught up with her father's career as a surgeon, as well as with my activities during these many years. As part of our conversation, Anne, his daughter, told me that she knew very little of her dad's past in Egypt where he was born, grew up, and studied medicine. This astonished me very much as her father was part of a very well-known and preeminent family in Egypt. So I proceeded to tell her all about her father's family and about his youth and studies when he lived in Egypt.

All through my talk and explanation with Anne, her eight-year-old daughter, Kendall, kept asking me questions about ancient Egypt, the pharaohs, and particularly about the queen pharaohs—Hatshepsut and others. Obviously, she was being taught this subject in school. I kept answering her questions as much as I could remember from my years in school, as well as from the common knowledge I had from growing up in Egypt. During the course of my conversation with the girl's mother, I learned that she, her husband, and Kendall lived in South Carolina.

I studied architecture in Egypt. And after immigrating to the USA, I got a couple of master's degrees relating to my profession and was practicing as an architect here in the States, in Washington, DC. Again in the course of our conversation, I told Anne and her husband that a couple of months later, I was scheduled to attend the AIA convention in Charlotte, North Carolina, where I had to give a talk on a subject I was very knowledgeable in. There, to my surprise, Anne's husband told me that they were living half an hour from Charlotte, North Carolina. That is in a city at the frontier between the two states. So I invited the three of them to have lunch with me when I would be in Charlotte. Before taking this trip, I purchased a small book on the Egyptian pharaohs for children her age.

When in Charlotte, we had a very pleasant lunch, the four of us, and throughout the lunch, Kendall was looking at the pages of her book and was asking me questions about this pharaoh or this queen, and I answered as well as I could. Anne asked me if her daughter could correspond with me via email, and I okayed that. She also asked me if Kendall could call me uncle, and I okayed that too. For quite a few months, we corresponded, and Kendall's questions were more and more, wanting to know more about the Egyptian life during the pharaonic time, and I found myself having to research more and more to answer her questions.

So I decided to write a book—a novel about an imaginary story taking place during this period. The novel was the vehicle for me to describe life in Egypt during this period. This novel was dedicated to Kendall and in memory of her grandfather. As she was sometimes referred to by her parents as a little princess, as many parents do, she thus became an Egyptian princess in the book.

Originally, I planned to write the book for children. But as I was writing, as she was growing up in age, and as I kept giving more details and information, I decided that this book should be for children of all ages—from eight years old to eighty years old. Enjoy. My goal is that all the little princesses who would read this book will enjoy reading it and will see themselves as the Kendall of this book.

Introduction

The story in this novel is totally the fruit of this author's imagination. As said in the preface, it resulted from conversations I had with a young girl related to me that I met at the wake of her grandfather to provide a description of the life in ancient Egypt.

I decided to first use a description of life in the palace of the pharaoh. This allowed the description of a pharaoh's palace, as well as some of the beautiful rooms that were used by large crowds. As the story developed, it allowed me to describe some of the important monuments built during the various dynasties of the pharaonic period. These descriptions did not take into account the different dynasties during which buildings, monuments, or temples were erected.

The novel's story is that of a pharaoh who had two sons. One was the heir to the throne, and the other was the son the pharaoh had with a princess, the daughter of the king of Syria. When the pharaoh was assassinated through a gift from the Syrian king, a group of Syrians gods plotted to replace the son who was the heir of the throne with the son of the Syrian princess, the widow of the assassinated pharaoh. These gods outsmarted the Egyptian gods and used a sorcerer to change the legitimate heir to the throne into a frog. This sorcerer told the frog that he could become human again if he would be kissed by an Egyptian princess, but he would have the chance to be kissed only once every one hundred years.

The frog wandered in Egypt for a long time, witnessing events and remembering them. As he was wandering in a port, he was curious about a container and got into it. This container was aboard a boat traveling to Europe and then to the United States. He kept being regenerated and wandered for a period of about thirty centuries. When in the United States, he found a child who was the daughter of a medical doctor of Egyptian descent. The frog told her that one of her grandfather's ancestors was a pharaoh and that therefore she was an Egyptian princess. After asking her several times to kiss him, she finally did, but very gingerly.

As soon as she did, the frog changed into an Egyptian prince. He was dressed as the son of a pharaoh, and he proceeded to tell her his story. He told her of his life in the palace of his father and how he was changed into a frog. He also told her how he had to be kissed by an Egyptian princess to become human again. Then he described life in the pharaoh's palace, and he described all the important buildings and monuments of the pharaonic period. He did this as he narrated his life as the pharaoh's son, as well as all the events he participated in. He told her all about his life as a human being, as well as what happened when he was turned into a frog. Then he described all the events that happened in the kingdom, as he was witnessing what was going there.

One event of particular importance in the novel is the story of a good-looking young man who was a laborer in the farm of a rich farmer. The wife of the farmer became interested in the young man, and she invited him to have fun with her. He refused and ran away from the farm, fearing the anger of the farmer and his wife. He landed in a forest not far from the farm and was helped by an old man with long hair and a long beard who called himself Old Man River. He was there as the result of a curse by a wicked sorcerer. The old man fed the young man and advised him to join the army to evade the vengeance of the farmer's wife. And that was what he did.

The young man excelled as a soldier and came up the ranks and led the pharaoh's armies to several victories. He did so by noticing a weapon of the enemy, copying it, and substantially improving it. His achievements were brought to the attention of the pharaoh, who asked that he be brought to him, and he elevated him to the rank of general. Remembering his humble upbringing and the fact that he was always barefoot, he decided to call himself Vas Nu Pieds. The general caught the attention of the pharaoh's sister, who fell in love with him. Thus the pharaoh decided that they should get married. The wedding ceremony is described in the novel, and he became the brother-in-law of the pharaoh.

When the pharaoh was assassinated, Vas Nu Pieds, helped by his men, immediately proceeded to kill all the serpents getting out of the urns as the pharaoh's body was taken by the priest for mummification. Vas Nu Pieds then helped Khouf, the son and heir of the pharaoh, to decide on the kind of mummification they wanted. Vas Nu Pieds, then realizing that the assassination of the pharaoh was a declaration of war by the king of Syria, went to his headquarters to immediately prepare his troops for war.

When the mummification process that took seventy days was underway, intense discussions were taking place to decide who would be the next pharaoh. As was narrated at the beginning of the synopsis, a group of Syrian gods replaced the son who was the heir of the throne with the son of the widowed Syrian princess of the assassinated pharaoh. A sorcerer changed the real heir to the throne into a frog and, as he did so, told the frog that once every one hundred years he would have the chance to become human again if he were kissed by an Egyptian princess.

From then on, the frog started to witness all that was going on in the kingdom and the mummification of his dad, as well as how the new heir was behaving. This guy, helped by his mom and the sorcerer Twistmind, who became the tutor of the new heir, invited all the kings and rulers from around Egypt to come for his coronation. That included the murderer of his dad.

When Vas Nu Pieds realized that the king of Syria was on his way to Egypt, he was waiting for him with his armed forces. A small group stayed with him, and the rest were hidden in strategic locations. When the king appeared with a small army with the intent of controlling Egypt, Vas Nu Pieds approached him and asked him to return to his country, as he was not welcome in Egypt. The king refused and proceeded to attack Vas Nu Pieds and what appeared to be a small group of soldiers. It did not take long for Vas Nu Pieds to defeat the king and take him as a prisoner.

He then turned back to the frontier of Egypt and waited for his half-brother, Syroman, who was coming to meet his grandfather at the frontier. When Vas Nu Pieds saw Syroman coming, he asked him where he was going. Syroman answered that he was going to welcome his grandfather, who was coming to Egypt to be there for his coronation. Vas Nu Pieds then arrested him for treason and let him join his grandfather. Vas Nu Pieds reentered Egypt with his two prisoners, directed himself first to Memphis, and from there directly to the pharaoh's palace in Thebes. There he arrested Merdonice, the daughter of the Syrian king, and her lover, Twistmind, again for treason. He took his four prisoners to the grand priest of Karnak to be judged according to the Egyptian laws. There he was named Pharaoh and took the name of Rameses XXIII.

The novel gives a description of the life during the pharaonic times, as well as the locations where such events took place. All the descriptions, as well as almost all the pictures illustrating this story, were generated from descriptions from the internet. If and when the author found pictures identified as copyrighted, such pictures were not included in this novel.

Many events in the story present beliefs that are the products of the author's imagination, such as mermaids, nilemaids, underwater kingdoms, and talks with animals. A belief in sorcery, however, has always existed. Finally, the novel wants to be, and is, a moral story. It emphasizes that crime does not pay, that criminals are caught, and that they pay for their crimes.

1 The Encounter

It happened like it was a dream, and it seemed that I woke up from this dream three years later. When I talked about it to my friends, they all opened their eyes big, but no one wanted to believe me. However, it happened. Now I will tell you my story as it happened. Please be indulgent with me as I am only an eight-year-old girl, and I want the whole world to know my story.

It all started on a Friday night. My grandpa promised to go fishing with me the next day, and I was all excited about it. He gave me, as a gift, a fishing rod, a couple of hooks, and some plastic worms, as well as a small book with lots of pictures that explained how to fish. I tried my rod with the hook as explained in the picture book. Then as I was in my bedroom, my dog, Mignonne (her name is "cute" in French), was with me. I explained to Mignonne what we would be doing the next day. As I was talking to her, she moved her head like she agreed with all that I was telling her. I went to bed and slept, dreaming of catching next morning lots and lots of fish.

I woke up early, very early on Saturday, and at 7:00 AM, Mignonne and I were ready, and the two of us were very excited. I was waiting for my granddad at the house door for our day trip of fishing.

The place around the lake where we went fishing was very quiet. The lake was like a mirror of glittering water. My grandpa and I each sat on a small piece of cloth that Grandpa brought with him, and he hooked the worm on my fishing rod's hook and showed me how to throw the hooked worm away from the shore of the lake. All the while, Mignonne was running around, barking at butter-flies and birds and chasing squirrels. I tried twice to throw the hooked worm away from the shore, and the third time, Granddad was happy with the way I did it. He did the same to his fishing rod. And now we waited for the fish to catch.

I was thinking about how many fish I would catch and how I would get my mom excited by how good I was at fishing. I was also looking at the beautiful butterflies of all colors flying around us. My dog started to bark and bark, and all along I was hearing my grandpa mumbling, looking at the grass. At first I did not pay attention to my granddad mumbling as

Mignonne was barking louder and louder. Then I looked again at what my grandpa was looking at, and I saw him talking to a frog.

"Grandpa, are you talking to a frog?" I asked.

He did not answer me. "Grandpa, are you talking to a frog?" I asked again.

He looked at me, and I could see in his eyes all the love he had for me. I felt that love and I said, "I love you, Grandpa." Then it sounded like the frog was talking.

Am I crazy? Frogs don't talk.

"Grandpa, is this frog talking to you?" I asked. And yes, I heard the frog answering me directly. I felt that the little animal was looking at me directly in my eyes.

"Yes, I am talking to the old man, and he does not answer me. Also, ask your dog to stop barking. He is annoying me. And why is your grandpa just mumbling 'Frogs don't talk. I must be dreaming' to himself?

"I am talking," said the frog. "And yes, what you see is a frog."

I thought I was dreaming too! Frogs really don't talk. But this frog was talking. And I could not stand that this little beast would lack respect for my grandpa, as well as for my dog.

I shouted to the frog, "Don't speak that way to my grandpa!" Oh my god, I found myself scolding the frog. Yes, I was scolding the frog for not being respectful to my grandpa and to my Mignonne. The frog then became very humble in his speech and apologized.

"Sorry, beautiful girl. I am sorry. I did not mean to lack respect for this man, your grandpa. But he is not listening to me and does not realize that I am for real. And I need his or your help. I want you to know that I also love dogs. I had one."

"You need help. Sorry, we don't feed frogs, and you are a frog. You say you had a dog. Ha ha ha, how can a frog have a dog?"

"Oh no," said the frog. "By the way, what is your name?"

"My name?" I answered. "Why would I give my name to a frog? This is crazy. Look, I am dreaming. Get lost. We are here and my opportunity to fish, not to socialize with a talking frog."

"Please, please tell me your name. And no, you are not crazy. I know frogs don't talk and frogs don't have dogs. But I don't know how to say that. Well, you hear me, I am talking. Now tell me, what is your name?"

As I was having all my attention on the frog, my grandpa looked for and found a small box. And coming from behind the frog, he caught him and briskly put him in the box and closed the lid as the frog was shouting, "No . . . no . . . don't do that to me!"

"Oh no," said the frog. "You are my chance, my only chance.

Grandpa turned to me and told me, "I am losing my sanity. I want other people to see that this frog talked, if indeed the frog talked." Now he said, "Back to fishing."

All the while, as we were fishing, the frog was jumping and shouting in the box. Fortunately, the box lid was well secured.

"Oops! Something is pulling my rod, Grandpa. Grandpa, it is pulling hard."

Grandpa came to my help, and the two of us pulled and pulled, and a wiggling fish was dangling at the end of the line.

"Wow, wow, I caught a fish, and it is big!" I shouted.

"Yes, it is a big fish," my grandpa said. And that was the first of many fish we caught that day.

Grandpa and I returned home with a basketful of fish. I was so proud to show my mom the four fish I caught. Grandpa caught another four. The eight fish we brought home would make a great dinner. Mom received us with a big smile, and I ran to her, shouting, "Mom, Mom, I caught four fish, and we have a frog that talks."

"Well, well, well," said my mom, laughing loudly. "Did you also fish the frog? And for God's sake, frogs don't talk."

"Mom, this frog talks, and Grandpa and you will hear

him."

"Go wash your hands as I prepare dinner, darling," said Mom.

Back refreshed and clean, I asked Grandpa if he showed the talking frog to Mom.

"No," he said, "I was waiting for you."

"OK," I said, and I took the box where the frog was and started to talk to the frog. "Hey, frog, talk to me now." Nothing. Not one sound came out of the box. "Come on, Froggy, talk to me. Tell me, how do you feel being in a box?" Again nothing, no sound. Grandpa started to think that the two of us were dreaming and that the frog really never talked. He opened the lid of the box, and the frog jumped out of the box and under the table. I ran after him and tried to catch him, but every time I was about to do it, he jumped out of my way. Then he found his way out of the door and into the garden. All my excitement about a frog that talked went out with the frog, and now I felt ashamed of believing that a frog could talk. But I could swear that frog talked to me, and it also talked to my grandpa. That night, I went to bed still thinking of the four fish I caught and of the adventure—as crazy as it sounded to me by then—of a talking frog.

When I was saying my prayer before sleeping, I heard a *psst psst* coming from under my bed. Here I was dreaming again. "I don't believe in the bed monsters anymore," I told myself. And bed monster it was not.

"Look here. This way." I heard a voice I recognized immediately.

Automatically, I looked at the direction of the voice, and there was the frog. "How on earth did you get there?" I asked. "Can't you take no for an answer?"

"Oh, pretty lady," he answered, "I am so sorry to just appear in your bedroom, but I need to be alone with you and talk seriously to you."

I kept thinking that I was either crazy or I was sleep-

ing and dreaming again of the frog, or that something really strange was happening. As I was thinking, I heard the frog kind of answering me by saying, "Yes, dear, something strange is happening. And yes, I am here with you for a purpose— a purpose I cannot tell you yet. I want you to trust me."

"To trust you? Come on, you are just a frog," I said to myself. And as he was reading my thoughts, he answered me back.

"Yes, I know. I am just a frog, but obviously not like any other frog. How many frogs do you know who speak like I am doing now? And look now. What do you think I have in my paws?"

"What do you have in your paws?" I asked myself.

"Does it look to you like a book?" said the frog.

"Oh yes, now that you say it," I answered.

"Do you know what it is?" said the frog.

"No," I answered.

"Look under your pillow where you save your diary. This is your diary. I am about to read from it if you don't listen to me."

"But that is so small a book," I said to myself.

It seems that the frog guessed my thoughts and answered me. "I am a frog. I cannot handle large objects. I reduced it in size to hold it, and if you don't listen to me, I will read it."

"You are blackmailing me, frog," I said.

"Oh no, Kendall. Don't take it this way. I just want your attention."

"You got it," I said. "How did you know my name, frog?"

"Oh, you shall know it soon." Then the frog jumped onto my bed, left the small book, and jumped back on the floor. In the meantime, the little book started to get back to its normal size.

The frog had a point. I knew of no frog that talked, and much less of frogs that read, know my name, and can reduce the size of a book to be able to read it.

I was confused. I read stories when I was a little girl of all kinds of animals. And in these stories, they all kind of talked to one another. But I knew, reading these stories, that these were just stories.

Here and now, this frog was for real. And this frog was talking to me. "What do you want from me?" I asked.

He answered me with a question—a question that he immediately answered himself.

"Is your grandpa from Egypt?" I did not have time to answer that. He answered his own question and said, "Yes, he is. I know it. You see, I know so much. You will have to trust me." "Trust you, Froggy? And why's that?" "Oops," the frog answered. "Please don't call me Froggy. That is offensive." "Offensive?" I said. "Why is that?" He did not answer this question but said, "Now I will ask you to close your eyes, and I will hypnotize you."

"What is that?" I asked.

"Ah," said the frog, "I will help you to sleep artificially. And by doing so, you will be able to see things that happened many years ago."

"Ha ha ha." I laughed. "You, little frog, will tell me what happened to me years ago?"

"No, not necessarily to you. Just look at me. Look at me directly to my small eyes. Yes, like that."

And as I looked at him, he told me he would take me now in my thoughts in a river shore, away, very far away from here.

"But I am in my nighties," I said jokingly.

"Yes, I know. Don't worry. Now, Kendall, here you are. Sit, my beautiful Kendall. Sit on that rock at the edge of the water and, yes, look at me. Yes, look at me as I grow and grow and grow."

Sure enough, the little frog started growing and growing and stood up facing me. The frog was now almost as tall as I am, and I sat and faced him. "Don't be scared, Kendall," he said. "I won't hurt you. I would like you to help me. I need your help, and I need it tonight. This is the thirtieth chance I have for my life to change. If you don't help me, it will take another one hundred years of vagabonding around the earth for me to get another chance."

In my condition of artificial sleep, whatever condition that was, I could still think, and I asked two obvious questions: "Why thirtieth chance and one hundred years each time?" Wow! That was lot of time. He was pulling my leg. "Pulling my leg," I told myself, but this is a frog, an animal. Maybe an animal that talked, but I could very well calculate one hundred times thirty is three thousand years.

I looked at the frog and said, "You mean to say you have lived for three thousand years, you little animal?"

The frog did not answer my question but asked me something with tears in his eyes—yes, I could see the tears in the frog's eyes. "Would you help me, please? Would you help me or not?"

"Help you with what?" was my answer.

"Well, Kendall, you have first to promise to trust me. I promise I will not hurt you, not at all. But if you help me, you will see what others around you never saw. Yes, I say never saw or will never see. You will feel wonders that others around you never felt or will never feel. You will—"

"Hey," I interrupted him. And being ironic, I asked, "What would I have to do to help you, Mr. Frog?"

"Oh," the frog answered, "you are calling me Mr. Frog. Thank you, thank you."

The frog was as tall as I was when sitting, facing the river. He then started to shrink and become less swollen till he returned to the normal size of a frog.

At this point, the frog told me, "Take me in your hands. Don't be scared. I won't hurt you, and your act of charity will be greatly appreciated."

"My act of charity! A frog in my hand would be an act of charity? All little boys catch frogs and play with them. I am not a boy, and I am not a little girl anymore."

Well, I picked up the frog and had him in my two hands. I have to admit, I was trembling, having this vicious little animal in my hand. But something in my mind was telling me, *Keep it there, Kendall. Keep it there. You don't want to hurt this animal.*

The little frog looked me in the eyes, and now he looked serious. With an expression of sorrow as if he were begging, he said, "I know what I am about to ask you to do, you will find disgusting. I know if I were you, beautiful lady, I will also feel disgusted to kiss a frog. But please, please kiss me. Just a little sweet kiss, Kendall. Please."

I felt hypnotized—now I knew what it meant to be hypnotized. I moved the frog toward me, and with disgust, my lips moved toward the frog, who by now was totally frozen in my hand. And almost automatically, with my eyes closed, I placed a silly little kiss on this animal. Suddenly, the whole room exploded in light. Then the room walls—all the walls—became colored in gold, like they were covered with real gold leaves. At first I was scared.

Then he faced me. I saw him starting to develop into a handsome young man. I thought at first that he was in a bathing suit. Then I realized that he was dressed as one of the Egyptian pharaohs or gods or whatever you would call the man I saw facing me. He was wearing a wrapped skirt of gold-and-blue cloth. He had a woven gold shirt and had a round bib around his neck that was woven in gold and light blue. He was also wearing bracelets around his arms, as well as around his wrist. And he had a wide gold-and-red scarf that went down his chest. He also had an elongated bonnet with the gold head of a snake in front of it and a black feather-like spiral above it.

He was barefoot. All in all, that man looked like those Egyptian pharaoh pictures that you see in books.

I was so stunned looking at him. I thought I was dreaming. Mignonne, my dog, was barking at this man and wanted to go and welcome him, but she could not move from where she was, like she was glued to the floor. I could not believe my eyes. I thought that these things were only in fairy tales—kiss a frog and here appears a handsome prince. I held my breath and closed and opened my eyes a few times, making sure I was awake and not dreaming. I pinched my arm till it hurt. Yes, I was awake, pretty much awake, but here he was, standing up in front of me.

Now he gently moved toward me slowly so as not to scare me, and as he moved, he talked to me. He mumbled words that I guessed were "thank you."

"Thank you very much, Kendall. You just undid a three-thousand-year spell. I know you just can't understand that just like this. But for the last three thousand years, I was turned by a wicked sorcerer and his witch friend into a frog. I wandered all over the world with a chance—only one chance—every one hundred years to try to undo their wicked action. I will tell you more about this and much more. But now, sweet and wonderful lady, I want to thank you for getting me back to what I always was— Prince Khouf Wan Aron, heir to the throne of Upper and Lower Egypt, whose throne was swindled by those two wicked beings to install their illegitimate son as the pharaoh.

"Now, Kendall, you have seen enough for a day. I will let you sleep and dream and be a happy, wonderful young princess, because you are one. And when you wake up tomorrow, I will let you see more and feel more of those marvelous things that you are entitled to have. Now *Wata bata rata*: all the blessings of all our gods of Egypt from Amun-Ra to Aton be bestowed upon you and your loved ones. You have once and for all established the right order of succession, even if this happened three thousand years later. I call on all of you, our gods, to bless this wonderful princess. Pharaohs of Egypt never die. They move from life on earth to eternal life."

After hearing those words, I went to sleep with Mignonne, my dog, next to me. That night, I dreamed of angels dancing all around me and my dog and of everyone dancing with joy. I was so happy, so happy.

2 Who Is Prince Khouf Wan Aron?

I woke up the next morning feeling my dog Mignonne's tongue over my face. She was licking my cheeks as she nestled very comfortably next to me. I opened my eyes and started to think about a frog that talked, a handsome Egyptian prince, and all the crazy talks I had during my dream. The more I was thinking about it, the more I realized that the frog, the handsome Egyptian prince, and all that occurred were not dreams. It all happened before I went to sleep.

"Could it be real?" I just kept thinking that if I talked about what happened, no one would believe me. Then whoever listened to me would think I was crazy. But I am used to sharing all my thoughts and all my feelings and anything I do with my mom. I kept no secrets from my mom. Still I was thinking that as a grown-up girl, if I told her what happened, she would think that I either made up this story or I just dreamed it during my sleep. But my grandpa also saw the frog. And the frog also talked to him.

"Good morning, darling," said my mom as she entered my room. She came to hug me and kiss me good morning. "Down!" she shouted to Mignonne, who did not like this order from Mom. Groaning, she obeyed and went down from my bed. "How did you sleep, darling?" my mom asked.

"I slept well, Mom. But something strange happened to me. I don't know if it happened before I went to sleep or in my dream." As I said this, I blushed.

My mom always knew when I said the truth or tried to disguise it. She noticed that my face was red by then. She said, "What are you trying to hide from me, baby?"

"Oh, Mom," I said. "Nothing. But what happened was so crazy. I don't know how to tell you about it."

"Just tell me, baby. You know how much I love you, and it does not matter what it is or what happened. I still love and will love you very, very much, darling."

"Remember that frog that Grandpa brought home yesterday, saying it talked to him? It also talked to me. This frog came back to my room last night when I was about to sleep. He talked to me again and somehow played tricks and convinced me to kiss him."

"You kissed a frog?" my mother interjected with an expression of disgust on her face.

"Yes, Mom," I answered with a meek face. "And that was when it all happened. Mom, when I kissed this frog, it was like magic happening. I know you may not believe it, but I'll never lie to you. Here is what happened. Maybe it was a dream, maybe not, but I saw it all, Mom.

"When I kissed the frog, my whole bedroom became colored in gold, Mom. It was real gold. It was then that I saw a handsome young man facing me. He was dressed as one of the Egyptian pharaohs or gods. I can tell you exactly how he was dressed, every detail, Mother."

"You were dreaming, darling," my mom said. "That is all right, and all of us dream sometimes. All of us have fantastic dreams. It is normal, Kendall."

"I am sure I was not dreaming, Mother. I was completely shocked. It was like I could tell you every single detail of what he was wearing, the sweet and loving smile he had for me, and how he talked to me once he turned into a prince from the frog he was."

"OK, darling. I want to believe you. Now, sweetheart, get up and get dressed and come and have breakfast."

"All right, Mom. But please, please believe me. It all happened for good."

My dad was waiting for me with a wide smile at the breakfast table, and he opened his arms, took me there, and hugged me and kissed me. Then he said, "So I see, darling. You lived a fairy tale in your dream."

"I was not dreaming, Dad. It really happened. Ask Granddad if that frog he brought home was talking to him. He will tell you, Dad."

I was by now frustrated that my parents did not believe my story and thought I was dreaming. Well, after all, I ended up telling myself, "Maybe I was indeed dreaming, and I should forget about this crazy dream." I was frustrated, but things being what they were, I just decided to forget about it and, even if not convinced, tell myself that "Yes, Kendall, it was only a dream."

All during the day, as I helped my mom do things around the house, I knew that it was one thousand years before our Lord Jesus Christ lived and that it was well before there was a Roman or a Greek empire. All that I learned in school. And then the story of a wicked witch and her sorcerer friend that turned people into frogs— that is what you read in fairy tales. These kinds of things don't really happen. Yes, I must have dreamed it all despite the fact it was so vivid. Well, he said he was Prince Khouf Wan Aron, heir to the throne of Upper and Lower Egypt. His throne was swindled by these two wicked beings who wanted to install their illegitimate son as the king. I'll have to go to a library and see if such a prince indeed existed. And if so, what really happened to him?

I went to play in our garden with my friends from the house next door. And I kept hearing, when I was playing, these words that kept resonating in my mind: "Wata bata rata. All the blessings of all our gods of Egypt, from Isis to Aton, be bestowed on you and your loved ones. I call on our gods to bless this wonderful princess. Pharaohs of Egypt never die. They move from life on earth to eternal life."

"Wow," I kept saying to myself, "no one ever dies."

The day went by, and after kissing my parents good night, I went to my bedroom, still thinking of my pharaoh dream. I went to bed, still not sure of myself anymore. Mom and Dad, whom I trust and love very much, almost convinced me that I was dreaming. "I must have been dreaming," I kept telling myself. As I was in my thoughts, Mignonne, my dog, jumped on my bed. Then as I was saying my prayers—I always pray before sleeping—I felt like I was going to sleep.

Suddenly, my bedroom exploded in light. Then the room walls, all the walls, became colored in gold, like they were covered with real gold leaves. I felt hypnotized, I could not move, and I was scared. Was I awake? Was I dreaming again? I could not tell anymore. Then, facing me, I saw starting to develop in front of me the same handsome man I saw last night. And yes, he was dressed as one of the Egyptian pharaohs or gods.

"Hello, Kendall. I am Prince Khouf Wan Aron. Yes, it was me that you kissed when you kissed that frog. And I owe it to you for freeing my soul from that frog. My real name, the one my parents used to call me, is Seth. And my very close relatives and my dad and mom used to call me Setty. That is the name I allow you to call me now that you freed my soul from the body of a frog.

"You should know that then, like today, we believed

that every one of us has a soul. We called our souls in ancient time the Ka, or the Kha. My soul went from generation to generation for more than three thousand years to a living frog, making me wander all over the world, hoping to have it freed and rejoin the souls of my ancestors in heaven. We ancient Egyptians believe in eternal life for our souls if we had lived a good life, according to our religion, and if all our deeds and what we did in our lives were right."

"Are you for real? Or am I dreaming again?" I said, almost as a whisper.

"Yes, I am for real, dear Kendall. Don't worry about that.

"Kendall! You wonderful Egyptian princess, I want you to know and bear witness when you grow up that what happened that made me change into a frog was a horrible act committed by a wicked sorcerer. Don't go and look for what I am going to tell you in a library. Unfortunately, what I am going to tell you was not recorded in the history of ancient Egypt, and that is because of what I will let you know now."

"Oh?"

"My father was the pharaoh known as Amenhotep the Great. He was a great conqueror, and he defended our country with courage and determination. He not only defeated any country that wanted to invade our dear Egypt but he also occupied it. And to make sure that peace was reestablished, he did what all great pharaohs did then. He married the youngest daughter of the Syrian prince that wanted to invade Egypt and made her one of his many wives. Her name was Merdonice, and she was quite young and very attractive."

"Many wives? You are saying that your dad had many wives? This is polygamy. Is this what pharaohs were doing? And how were they satisfying all these women?"

"In the old times, it was current and normal for a pharaoh to have many wives. And how were they satisfying all these women? Ha ha ha, I don't know, Kendall. Maybe they were not doing so.

"I was the eldest son of the pharaoh, and my mother was his first wife. And she was the only one that could use the title of queen.

"My father died suddenly, and I was too young to be immediately named as the new pharaoh. The court named a priest, whose name was Twistmind, as my tutor. This priest was a dishonest person—a sorcerer with a twisted mind."

"What is a tutor, Prince Khouf?"

"Don't call me prince, please, Kendall. A tutor, my sweet Kendall, is a person who can take care of a minor's education and welfare. This priest was supposedly taking care of my education as I was growing up, and he was trusted with preparing me to be a good pharaoh. In the meantime, the court named a temporary person to govern in my name until I would be of age to be officially govern-

PICTURE OF A PAPYRUS SHOWING THE OFFERING A GIFT TO A GODDESS

ing as the pharaoh of Egypt, my beloved country.

"It turned out that when my father was away fighting enemies of Egypt south of the country, Twistmind, the man who as you know now became my tutor, became a very close friend of Merdonice when my father passed away. Remember she was my father's new wife and was the daughter of the conquered Syrian prince. This princess became pregnant and had a son by Twistmind

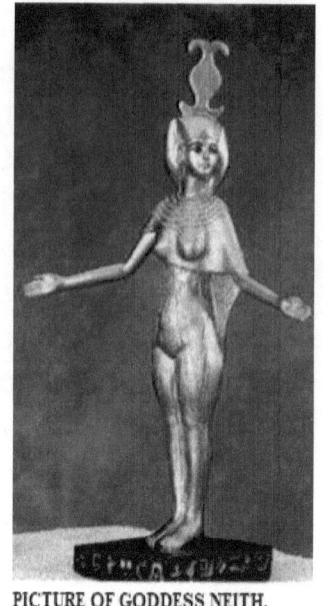

PICTURE OF GODDESS NEITH, GODDESS OF WAR AND HUNTING

Thoth, God of Wisdom

"Wow!" said Kendall. "That is horrible."

"Yes, indeed. And no one could explain how that happened. My father, who was a very generous man, did not ask questions. And he kept the baby as a member of his family. Although he was not sure it was his son.

"Later on, when my dad passed away, that tutor of mine and Merdonice, the Syrian wife of my dad, wanted this child, my half-brother, to put a claim to the throne of Egypt. This could not be done according to the laws of Egypt.

"All my troubles started here. Let me explain to you the whole story, Kendall. In order to understand what I

PICTURE OF GOD BAAL, SYRIAN GOD OF THUNDER

am about to tell you, you have to know that three thousand years ago, things were very different from what they are now in your world. Our religion had many gods—hundreds of them. We had a god of wisdom, the god creator of the world, the goddess of war and hunting, and the god of love. Many of the gods were good gods, and some were evil gods. Some of the gods were much more powerful than others, and often the less powerful gods would kind of beg the powerful gods to help them in achieving what they wanted."

"You mean to say that these gods made of stone could talk to one another

"No, my dear princess. Stones do not talk. What was made of stone was a representation of these gods. OK, listen. In order for you to get the picture on how these gods related to one another, you may compare them somehow to the saints and angels of the Christian religion that you practice now. Most of these gods were taking the forms of living beings—human or animals—and sometimes they would have a human body with a bird or other animal head. You see, they were not made of stone. They would talk to people and intervene in their lives. In a moment, I will introduce you to the gods that were involved with me and with my claim to become the pharaoh of Egypt.

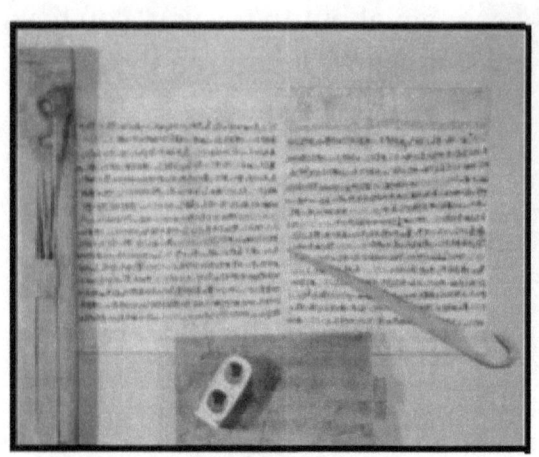

PAPYRUS WAS A PLANT THAT COULD BE PROCESSED TO BE USED AS PAPER. THIS PICTURE SHOES A SHEET OF PAPYRUS ,A PEN AND A SMALL POT OF INK

"First, my darling little friend Kendall, let me tell you more of my life as a boy, as the son of the pharaoh, then as I turned into a young man and was prepared in my father's palace to govern my country. I was born in the city of Memphis. This city used to be very close to where the actual city of Cairo is located. Memphis was the capital city of my ancestors. Later, when new dynasties of pharaohs came to power and there were twenty-eight dynasties in our history, the capital was moved from Memphis to the city of Karnack. This city is where the actual city of Luxor is located now. If you look at a map of Egypt, you would locate easily these two cities. I was born in Memphis because when my mom was due to give birth to me, she was visiting family and friends there. Since I was the son of the pharaoh, I had to be protected from the bad gods that may have wanted to harm me. So until they could provide me with full protection the son of the king must have, my mom and her family hid me in the papyrus marshes.

"Just in case you don't know, the papyrus is a plant that used to grow in abundance in Egypt. It was used to make paper, where the scribes—these were the people who knew how to write and read in ancient Egypt—wrote what was important to the kingdom. Often, as you know, most people today refer to them as old Egyptian."

GODDESS ISIS
GODDESS OF MARIAGE, FERTILITY AND MOTHERHOOD

"Your mom and her family hid you in the papyrus marshes like what happened to Moses in the Bible?" asked Kendall.

"Yes, Kendall. That was a known practice then. Now let's get back to my birth, depending on the magic of the goddess Isis for protection. This was a very powerful goddess in our history.

"My mom and her family planned my trip back to where my dad, the pharaoh, lived. That was in Karnack. The trip from Memphis to Karnack was a big affair then. They had to have a royal boat for my mom and me and several other boats which would precede and follow

THIS IS HOW A SCRIBE LOOKED LIKE

the royal boat for protection. Here is a picture of a model of the royal boat that we took to go from Memphis to Karnack."

"How big was this boat? The model you are showing me seems quite small for a queen and her suite, as well as for her son and his nanny and other help."

"Except for my mom, my nanny, and a friend or two who were in the main boat, the remaining people of my mom's suite were in other boats."

"Oh, I see," I said. "Please continue."

"Along the Nile River and any place where our boats were passing by, the people would come and greet us and shout, 'Long life to the pharaoh's son!' When we finally arrived in Karnak, my dad, the pharaoh, and all the royal court were waiting for us, and we were received with full honors, lots of musicians, and dancers. And all kinds of the priests of the temple and just ordinary people greeted us.

"Also in the same palace were the other wives of my father, and that included the daughter of the king that wanted to invade Egypt. Remember I told you about her and about the son she had. The palace of the pharaoh was a very large place with several houses, all of them connected to one another. There were very large rooms where my father would receive the ambassadors, the grand priests, and all the important people of his administration. I will tell you more of how the pharaoh and his family lived in the palace later on in our talk.

"My father died suddenly."

"How did your dad die? Was he very old? Or was he a sick man?

"No, sweet princess. My dad was murdered by a gift of the king of Syria."

"A gift killed your dad? How is that? Was that gift poisoned?"

"No, Kendall. The so-called gift was an urn with snakes with very potent poison. When my dad opened the urn's cover, a very venomous snake bit my dad, and he died immediately. When this happened, I was too young to be immediately named as the new pharaoh. A tribunal of gods named a tutor to take care of me.

"What is a tutor?"

"A tutor is person who should take care of my education and welfare as I was growing up and prepare me to be a good pharaoh."

"Who would govern the country in the meantime?"

"In the meantime, the tribunal of gods named a temporary person to govern the country in my name until I would be of age to officially claim the kingship of Egypt and become the new pharaoh of Egypt, my beloved country."

"Back to what I was telling you. When my dad passed

Thoth, God of Wisdom

away, my tutor, Twistmind, and Merdonice, the Syrian wife of my dad, claimed that her son, my half-brother, Syroman, was to become the new pharaoh."

"How can that be? His mom was Syrian."

"That was it. This was impossible since this boy's mother was not Egyptian by birth, and the pharaoh, at this time, had to have an Egyptian-born father and mother.

"By dying, my dad joined the gods of Egypt, and my mom immediately claimed the kingship of Egypt for me, as it was customary to do so. She put that claim to a tribunal of the major gods. This tribunal was presided by the sun god, Amun-Ra, of the city of Heliopolis.

"Thoth, the god of wisdom, told the sun god, Amun-Ra, that I should have the Sacred Eye immediately. It was the symbol of the cosmic order of justice and of

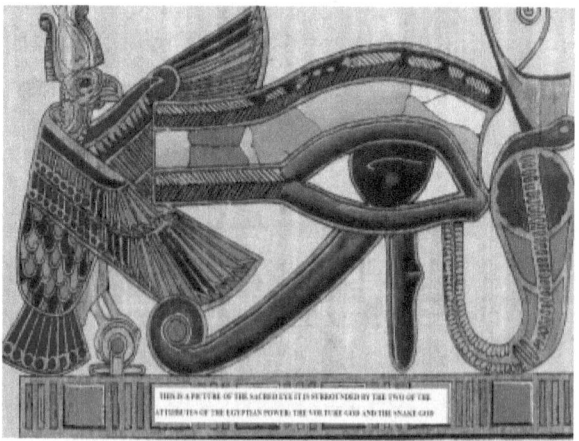

kingship. Every pharaoh or pharaoh-to-be must receive the Sacred Eye to be considered a pharaoh. The god Shu urged the immediate approval of me becoming the next

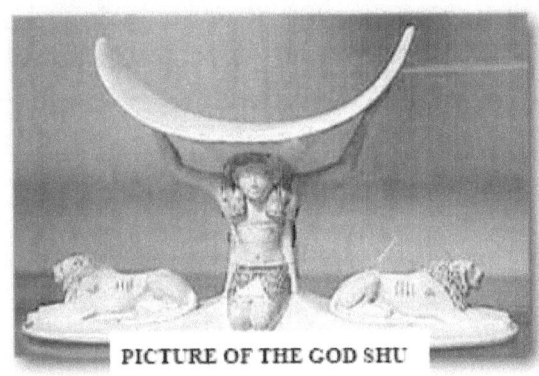

PICTURE OF THE GOD SHU

pharaoh. The god of wisdom, Thoth, confirmed that approving me as the next pharaoh was a million times right. Immediately, everybody in the palace of the pharaoh become very happy." That sounds great," said Kendall.

THE SUN GOD AMUN RA

"Well, yes, but the god Amun-Ra stopped this happiness short when, for some reason, he declared that he did not agree for me to possess the royal name ring, the cartouche."

"What is a cartouche?" asked Kendall.

"A cartouche was, in ancient Egypt, like a coat of arms that every pharaoh must have to be the pharaoh. It should have two of the five names that each pharaoh has. A good example is in the picture I am projecting for you.

PICTURE OD AN EGYPTIAN ROYAL CARTOUCHE

"The god Amun-Ra suggested that I and my half-brother, Syroman, the son of Merdonice, the foreign princess that my father married, should go out and have a hand-to-hand fight. The god Amun-Ra was not impressed and preferred very much that I not be named the next pharaoh immediately."

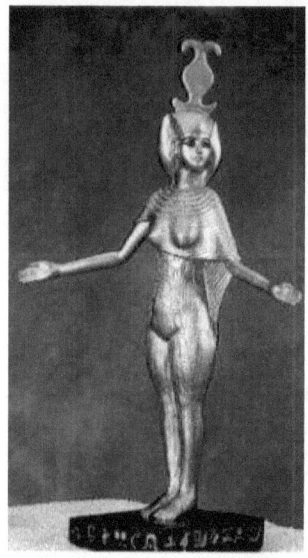

PICTURE OF THE GODDESS NEITH

"Why is that, Khouf?"

"It appeared later that the god Amun-Ra was very much manipulated by the foreign princess and her entourage of sorcerers and witches, who wanted to trick the gods into naming my half-brother as the pharaoh. This was despite the fact that almost everyone in the palace knew that this boy was not my father's son and that he was considered as my half-brother out of my father's generosity."

"So what happened then?"

"The council of gods decided then to end the discussion by sending a letter to the great creator goddess Neith, seeking her advice.

Goddess Neith replied that I should become the pharaoh. She also suggested that some gifts be given to the Syrian god Baal and the Syrian goddess Reshep. These two were also a sorcerer and a witch.

"The god Baal and the goddess Reshep did not want to accept this decision and refused any gifts from me."

"Then what?"

"The Syrian god Baal personally dared me to go and have a hand-to-hand fight with my half-brother, Syro-

PICTURE SHOWING A GROUP OF GODS HONORING & TALKING TO EACH OTHERS

man. I was so offended in my pride that I wanted to fight and show that I could and would win this fight and that I could win any fight since all the council gods, except the god Baal and the Syrian goddess Reshep, were with me, backing me."

"And?"

"Was I wrong, Kendall. I went out for the fight without knowing that the Syrian god Baal took a form that looked exactly like Syroman, my half-brother. We started the

fight, and it seemed that I was about to win this fight. It was then that the god Baal used his magic illegally, and I found myself slowly being transformed into a frog.

"You can imagine how furious I was. The spell was taking hold, and there was nothing I could do to change that. The other gods did not know what happened to me. And even if they knew, it was too late for them to undo the spell. Once assured of his victory and his control, the god Baal suppos-

PICTURE OF THE SYRIAN GOD BAAL

edly wanted to appear nice and assured me that every one hundred years, I would have the opportunity to become human again; that is, if for a few days at that time, a beautiful Egyptian princess would kiss me. And she would have to do that without knowing who I was. That way, when I became human again, I could die normally and rejoin my fathers and all the pharaohs of my dynasty in the eternal life."

"What happened after this horrible act? You must have felt terrible. Oh god, my poor friend, I can imagine."

"Then the god Baal returned to the council of gods and told them that it was too late for me to become the pharaoh, as I was killed in a fight in the forest and that a lion ate me. He lied and said that when he arrived to try to save me, I was gone as a meal for the lion and his family."

"Oh my god! What a horrible man this was."

"Yes, he was a real hypocrite, as he wanted to appear that he was so sorry for what happened to me. That was the way the imposter son of my father's Syrian wife was named the pharaoh, and I had to wander for thirty centuries as a frog from one generation of frogs to another."

"Thirty centuries—that means three thousand years, my poor prince."

"Yes, indeed, Kendall, my beautiful Egyptian princess. And you did not know till now that you were a princess—the princess that saved me. And you also did not know that your dad's family directly descended from royal Egyptian blood. Even if by now no one knows or gives importance to who we are and what your genealogy is, it remains that this is where you came from. And, princess, you are beautiful, gracious, and so sweet and nice."

"Thank you."

"You did for me a very nice, sweet act of compassion, and by doing so, you undid the wicked god-spell. For that, sweet princess, you will be rewarded in ways you never imagined. I will let you know all about the history of our great country, of our great civilization, and of our people throughout the ages. You will know, through me and with my guidance, many things and events that no one has yet discovered."

"And then what?"

"Then I will inspire you and guide you for you to become a very great and famous archeologist."

"What? How's that?

"How's that? That will be by showing you around all the secrets of the ancient Egyptian civilization. I will do that for you in a way that you will not have to lie to anyone, including your parents, because when I will talk to you, you will feel like you are dreaming, and you will remember your dreams and make them become reality."

"Thank you. Thank you very much. And when would these wonderful things happen, if ever?"

"Yes, they shall happen. I will start to make them happen, my darling princess, the next time I am with you. I shall be describing daily life as it was in ancient Egypt and, naturally, life as it was in my father's house, which was known as the pharaoh's palace. And that was before I became a frog. And I will also tell you how the pharaoh related to his people and the Egyptian people related to the pharaoh. That will be in our next conversation, my darling friend."

3 Life in the Pharaoh's Palace

"Hello, my sweet Kendall. As I promised you, you will see me now. You will feel as if you were dreaming."

"Are you hypnotizing me?"

"No, sweetheart. I am not hypnotizing you. What I am doing is simply making you feel that you are dreaming so I could make you feel and visualize all that I will tell you about life in Egypt—when I was growing up there as the pharaoh's son in the pharaoh's palace.

"To start with, I want to describe my life as a kid in my parents' house that is also the pharaoh's palace. This was not a regular-sized house like yours. It was a very large place with many, many different rooms within it. To give you an idea of how big it was, just imagine a football field with hundreds of rooms inside it. These rooms were grouped according to the various activities that took place within them."

"What does it look like?"

"I have a schematic plan of this palace. I shall project it on the wall of your bedroom for you to follow what I am describing. Can you see it now?"

"Yes, I do."

"My granduncle, the pharaoh Amenophis III, built the palace where we were living in. Give me your hand, Kendall."

"OK."

"Now let me guide you through the palace where I was born and where I grew up. Look at the plan of this palace. You can see that this plan was divided into two large longitudinal areas separated by a very long corridor."

"Yes, I can see that."

"On the upper side of this corridor were the private

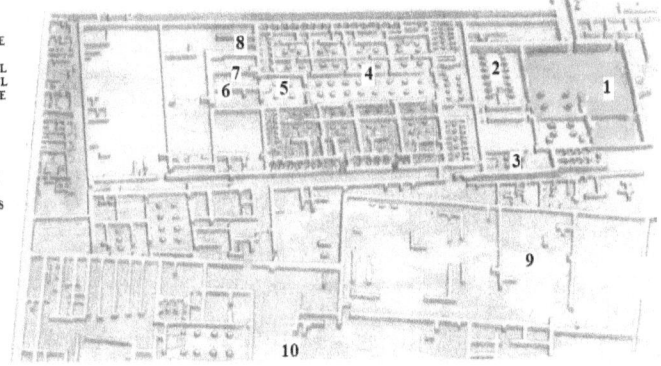

THE PALACE OF AMENOPHIS III AT MALQATA, NEAR THE CITY OF THEBES

LEGEND
1- VERY LARGE AUDIENCE HALL
2- LARGE AUDIENCE HALL
3- SMALL AUDIENCE HALL
4- ANTECHAMBER OF THE GREAT HALL OF THE HAREM
5- THRONE ROOM
6- BATHROOMS
7- ANTECHAMBER TO THE KING'S BEDROOM
8- KING'S BEDROOM
9- KITCHENS & SERVANTS QUARTERS
10- SOUTH PALACE

quarters of the pharaoh and his family. On the left side of these quarters were the pharaoh's family rooms. In these rooms lived his wives, children, and other members of his family. On the right part of the upper side of the corridor are the three audience halls where the pharaoh would often meet his subjects and the members of his administration.

"Is it OK so far?"

"Yes, I can see what you are describing."

"On the lower side of the palace plan, just under the corridor, were the offices of the members of the pharaoh's administration. These members were the officials who assisted the pharaoh in governing the country. On the right part of the lower side of the corridor was the kitchen where food was prepared for the pharaoh's family, as well as for the senior members in the pharaoh's administration. Next to the kitchen were the quarters where the servants of the palace lived."

"So far so good."

"South of the king's palace was a set of smaller statues of the gods Amun-Ra and Re-Harkhiti in the pharaoh's private rooms. I am projecting a picture of these statues. Can you see them?"

"Yes, I do."

"Several of the officials who worked in the king's palace lived in these buildings. Among them were army generals and members of the king's administration. I will not further describe these buildings. Suffice to say that these were the places where important members of the pharaoh's government, who had to be in constant contact with the king, had to live with their immediate families. OK?"

"Yes. OK."

"Now let's get back to the main palace of my dad, the pharaoh. And let us look at each one of the rooms there. Remember, Kendall, that the left part of the upper part of the palace was the immediate quarters of the pharaoh and of his family. Look at the plan. The pharaoh had his own bedroom. This is room No. 8 in the plan. Next to his bedroom was an antechamber. The antechamber is room No. 7 in the palace plan."

"What is an antechamber?"

"An antechamber or anteroom is a room where the servants of the pharaoh had access as they prepared his clothing or whatever they had to do to serve or please the pharaoh.

"I am taking out the statues of the gods Amun-Ra and Re-Harkhiti, and I am replacing it with a picture showing how a family lived during the time I was growing up in my father's palace."

"I see only women there in the picture. Why?"

PICTURE SHOWING FAMILY LIFE IN EGYPT DURING THE PHARAOH TIMES

"Remember, I told you that the women's quarters were separated from the men's quarters. But that does not mean that the women and men did not join one another for meals or other family activities.

"There were seven servants and a pygmy attached to the pharaoh's personal service. One was to prepare and keep his schedule up-to-date. Another was his personal secretary, and the five remaining ones were to take care of his clothing and other requirements, such as bringing him his meals if he wanted to eat alone or bringing him snacks or serving as go-between for him and members of his direct family. These servants were directly attached to his personal service and had nothing to do with the affairs of ruling the country. Next to the antechamber was the pharaoh's bathroom."

"I did not know that they had bathrooms so far away in history. In France, even King Louis XIV did not have such rooms in his palace in Versailles. He had to do it in a potty. Wow, can you imagine that?"

"Yes, darling Kendall, we had bathrooms then. And the bathrooms looked different from today's bathrooms, but they had pretty much the same use as yours have today.

"Part of the sets of rooms directly at the service of the pharaoh was the throne room. The throne room is room No. 5 in the palace plan. The throne room was in fact a very private small chapel dedicated to the god Amun-Ra. This was the room where the pharaoh went to have a private audience with the gods. Sometimes, he would ask the grand priest (someone like the pope of the Catholic Church) to meet him there so that they also meet with the gods. The pharaoh would invite the most intimate members of his administration to meet with him, either alone or in very small group, in an adjacent room very close to the throne room."

"A small room adjacent to the throne room?"

"Yes, and it was the greatest privilege for anyone to be invited to meet the pharaoh in this room. The reason for that was that this room was very close to the throne room.

"Among the servants that my dad had was a pygmy."

"A pygmy?"

"Yes, a pygmy. The pygmy attached to my father's group of servants was named Deneg. Deneg was originally from Central Africa."

"How did your dad get this pygmy from Central Africa?"

"He was given to the pharaoh by

THE THRONE ROOM

a victorious general as a gift. "This pygmy was a dancer, an acrobat, and a magician. His role was to entertain the pharaoh and his family. We all valued him and respected him as he was very nice and knowledgeable in the art of magic. He lived with his wife in a room not too far from my father's bedroom.

"We often went near his room, curious as kids were, to see him. As we were there and talked to him, he would say 'abracadabra' and poof... we found ourselves suddenly in a room with everything colored in pink, and the room was full of mini sized angels dancing all around. He would pick up an angel, give it to me, and again poof, the angel became a big ball of light. Suddenly, again, all the mini sized angels became doves. The doves were flying all around us by the dozen."

"Hey, hey, stop it. That cannot be."

"Yes, it can be, and it was. I don't know how to explain this. Maybe it was an illusion."

"Oh! OK then. And what else?"

"He would ask me to catch one of these doves. And as soon as I thought I did catch one, this dove became a monkey, and the monkey was laughing at me and playing all kinds of tricks on me. Then the monkey would puff at my eyes, and I would find myself flying all around with the doves. Wow, I could not believe it. Yes, I was flying like a dove."

"You? Flying like a dove? No way!"

"Yes, then another poof from our friend the pygmy and I was again myself in his room as if nothing had happened. You will understand that Deneg the pygmy became a very important person in the court, as my dad loved to have him around and kept him in great respect. Kendall, I loved watching Deneg's magic."

"Yes, I understand this, Khouf. How did this guy look?"

"You can see in the picture above a sculpture of Deneg the pygmy with his wife and his two children.

"Back now, Kendall, to the rooms in the palace. Here, very close to the pharaoh's bedroom and antechamber, are the quarters where my mom and I lived. As you can see, these quarters were located on the left side of the palace. This was the most privileged area after the pharaoh's own and very private quarters. That was because I was his eldest son and the heir to the throne of Egypt. Let me locate this area for you in the plan of the palace. This is the area that is colored in yellow. I lived there with my mom.

"We had about ten servants who also lived with us in these quarters."

"Ten servants for the two of you? Wow, what did they do?"

"These servants took care of the two of us. They cooked for us, they cleaned house for us, and they took care of our clothing and laundry. They also did all kinds of tasks that were required by the protocol of the pharaoh's palace. One of the servants was totally taking care of me. She would take care of all my needs. She would take care of my food and of everything that I would have to do. She would instruct the other servants to make sure that I would be, as the prince and heir to the throne of Egypt, well-groomed for my future functions."

"Wow, a servant that totally takes care of you and would take care of all your needs."

"Oh, I forgot to tell you. I also had several teachers who were in charge of my education. I was taught math, history, geography, religion, literature, and lots of other subjects that I had to learn in order to become a good pharaoh. Another thing I was also taught was to ride a horse and drive a horse carriage. I had to learn to ride a horse with and without a saddle. My instructor would often instruct the horse to run crazily as I was riding it, and I had to keep controlling the horse in any of these exercises.

"One thing you are not used to in today's world was that my dad, the pharaoh, had several wives. He also had many children by these wives, and he loved them all. But I was the most important for the country, as I was the heir to the throne. He also had many women who lived with and around these wives. These women were either related to his wives, friends of them, or were there because the pharaoh wanted them there or they were simply the servants of all these women. Several of these wives were foreign-born and were daughters of other kings or princes ruling other countries or provinces of Egypt."

"Did these women speak the Egyptian language?"

"Many of the women who were the servants of the foreign princesses knew two languages—the Egyptian language and the language of the princesses' country."

"That was not nice. The so-called princesses were therefore like objects that were gifted to the pharaoh."

"They were given to the pharaoh as wives to promote good will between the two countries, as was the custom during this time. As I told you before, one of these women was the one who wanted her son to become the pharaoh and was the cause of my demise, as you remember."

THE PALACE OF AMENOPHIS III AT MALQATA, NEAR THE CITY OF THEBES

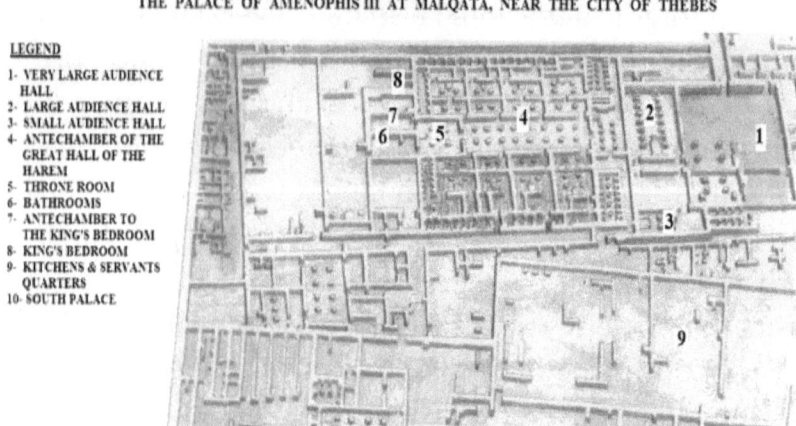

LEGEND
1- VERY LARGE AUDIENCE HALL
2- LARGE AUDIENCE HALL
3- SMALL AUDIENCE HALL
4- ANTECHAMBER OF THE GREAT HALL OF THE HAREM
5- THRONE ROOM
6- BATHROOMS
7- ANTECHAMBER TO THE KING'S BEDROOM
8- KING'S BEDROOM
9- KITCHENS & SERVANTS QUARTERS
10- SOUTH PALACE

"The area where these women and their children lived was called the harem. The harem was divided into two major areas, separated by a great hall. The foreign princesses, their children, and their servants and friends lived in one area, and the blood princess related to the pharaoh, their children, and their servants and friends lived in the other area. A large hall, where the women would socialize among themselves and may also have meals together, separated these two areas."

"Socializing among themselves? What did they do? Did they play cards? Ha ha ha."

"No, look at the picture I have for you. It shows a wom-

THIS PICTURE SHOWS TWO WOMEN DANCING AS THE OTHER WOMEN ARE CLAPPING THEIR HANDS AND ONE IS PLAYING AN INSTRUMENT TO PROVIDE MUSIC AND RHYTHM.

an playing an instrument to provide music and rhythm. It also shows two women dancing, and the other women are clapping their hands."

"Ah, thanks for the info."

"The women who lived in the pharaoh's harem often danced among themselves as a way to distract themselves, but also for celebrating the regeneration of the body. My mom often joined them. They all performed a dance called the offering table dance. This dance was symbolic and was to invite the people who died and were born in a new life to their first meal in heaven. There were also other dances. The most famous of them was a dance associated with the childbirth ceremony.

"Here again, sometimes out of nowhere, the pygmy Deneg would do some magic. As the women danced, they would all of a sudden see dogs and cats dancing with them. Some women would panic and shout, and before they knew it, there were no more dancing dogs and cats. They could not understand what was going on, and some thought that the spirits of the dead people joined them in dancing. Deneg would tell us about it in secret, and we would all laugh at this situation.

"Come on, my sweet Kendall. Let me take you through the palace plan again. Look there, at the area between the quarters where my mom and I were living and the pharaoh's private quarters.

There are several rooms (see plan legend), one room south of room 6 was a school for all the pharaoh's children, the other to the left of rooms 6 and 7 was the place where all the children of the pharaoh socialized and played between classes. I was authorized to play and socialize with all my half-brothers and sisters, but my schooling was to be alone for most of the courses. And I had special tutors to prepare me for my future functions.

"On the extreme right end of the palace were the three audience halls. These halls were where the pharaoh would hold audience with the officials of his administration, with visiting princes, or with delegates from foreign countries."

"Now what?"

"Now, my sweet Kendall, that I showed you what was happening in the part of the pharaoh's palace where my dad and his family lived, let me take you to the south part of the palace. This is the lower part in the palace plan. This area was exclusively used for offices for the officials

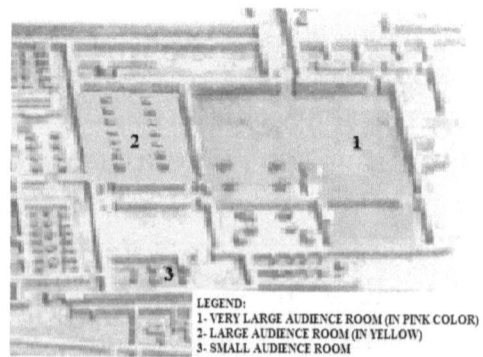

LEGEND:
1- VERY LARGE AUDIENCE ROOM (IN PINK COLOR)
2- LARGE AUDIENCE ROOM (IN YELLOW)
3- SMALL AUDIENCE ROOM

PART OFTHE AMENOPHIS III PALACE AT MALKATA NEAR THE CITY OF THEBES of the pharaoh's government, and the extreme right part of this space was the kitchen where the meals for all the people that worked there was prepared."

"Who were these officials?"

"Ha, I knew you would ask me this question. Kendall, I knew you would ask me this question. So let me tell you how the pharaoh ruled the country. By now you know that the king, my dad, sat at the top of the social order. Then directly reporting to him was a small group of top officials. The most important people of this group were two grand viziers, a grand priest, the military chief of the Egyptian Armed Forces, and the head of the scribes."

"Who was the boss of whom?"

PICTURE OF A VISIR

"One of the two grand viziers was the representative of the pharaoh for the southern part of Egypt, which we called Upper Egypt. The other grand vizier was the representative of the pharaoh for the northern part of Egypt, which we called Lower Egypt. There were many others viziers, all of them reporting to the two grand viziers."

"OK."

"One of these viziers was responsible for overseeing the treasury, and another was responsible for the granary, and again another was responsible for collecting the taxes. Maybe another dozen or so of viziers were there with similar responsibilities. You may ask me what a vizier looks like. I inserted a picture of a statue of a vizier for you to see for yourself. As you can see, a vizier looked very pompous and very important. As you may have studied in the Bible, Joseph, the son of Jacob, who was sold by his brothers in Egypt, was named by the pharaoh as his grand vizier. Let me tell you something funny that I still remember."

"OK, tell me."

"I still remember that one time, one of the viziers got really drunk and did not know where he was. He crawled to the pharaoh's suite of rooms, thinking he was going home. When he tried to kiss the pharaoh good night, thinking that the pharaoh was his wife, the pharaoh's guards caught him and immediately gave him a cold shower."

"Whoa! I thought they were going to kill him."

"No, no killing. That woke him up. Suddenly, he found himself all wet, facing the pharaoh. Realizing his situation, he ran away through the palace. That was funny, and all who saw him laughed their heads off."

"The grand priest of Egypt was a very important person. For you to see how important he was, just imagine the Catholic Church pope. He had direct access to the pharaoh and headed hundreds of priests from the temples all over Egypt."

"The pope! How's that? There were so many gods then. What was the role of an Egyptian priest?"

"The Egyptian priests in the pharaoh's time had a role different from the role of a priest in modern society. This was because the Egyptians did not practice any form of organized religion as we understand it now. The priests in ancient Egypt did not preach, tried to convert people to

THIS PICTURE SHOWS A PRIEST PERFORMING A
RELIGIOUS RITUAL TO THE THE GOD AMUN-RE

any religion, or cared for any group of people. They were not preaching, and there was no single holy book for the

Egyptians to believe in. In fact, Egyptian beliefs were based on various contradictory myths and legends surrounding the gods, and these were incompatible with any coherent system of belief. Look at the picture I have for you. It shows a priest performing a ritual for the god Amun-Ra. There's no explanation for what this ritual was."

"So what were the beliefs of the people? Let me know more."

"Here. Let me give you another example of the belief of the people at this time, Kendall. One myth described the sun traveling across the sky, ferrying the god Amun-Ra in his sacred solar boat. Every pharaoh, once deceased, hoped to join the divine crew of this boat when resurrected in the afterlife. The Egyptians also believed in another myth.

That was that the sun was born each morning on the eastern horizon to the sky goddess, Nut, and traveled across the vault of heaven, which was her body, to be swallowed by her at sunset on the western horizon."

"Really! Do all people believe this stuff?

"Yes, they do. A third myth they also believed in was that a giant scarab beetle, the god Khepri, pushed the fiery ball up

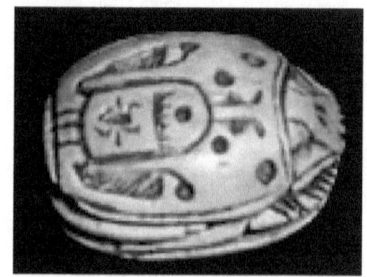

through the horizon at dawn and rolled it across the sky. You get the picture? And there were many other myths the Egyptian believed in."

"Yes, I do. What about the military? How did the pharaoh deal with them?"

"The military chief of the Egyptian Armed Forces was the head of the armed forces of Egypt. He was generally a famous general who got in this position after winning many battles against the enemies of Egypt, or he could also have inherited this position from his dad, with the consent of the pharaoh. Generals were always riding a chariot when they went to battle. The picture above shows a general on his chariot about to use his bow and arrow. The army of Egypt consisted of volunteers and of conscripts."

"Conscripts?"

"Let me tell you what a conscript is now that you asked me. A conscripted person is a person recruited for military service. The military service provided a means for promotion for the most humble villagers. Thus, if a villager showed valor in battle, he would get a military decoration, and the pharaoh would grant him a

piece of land. This land would be his and would be inherited by his descendants."

"That is great. The pharaoh was really very generous."

"Yes, he was. Valiant military men were also frequently chosen to fill top civilian and priest posts. The picture shown here shows a group of Egyptian soldiers in formation, ready to go to a battle. Notice that each soldier had a spear and a large shield to protect him from the enemy arrows and spears. Egyptian soldiers were considered the bravest in battle and were very much feared by their enemies. A large number of soldiers were lodged around the pharaoh's palace to protect him from enemies either within the palace plotting against him or from foreign enemies appearing unexpectedly.

"The pharaoh's palace had a large number of scribes. The head of the scribes was an important person in the palace. A scribe in Egypt, my dear Kendal, was a person who knew how to read and write well. Since we did not have schools at this time where children would go and learn how to read and write and learn other important knowledge that you, Kendall, have today in your country, scribes would learn their skills in their family. A father would teach his son. And sometimes, in small villages, a scribe would take pupils and teach them to read and write. Scribes were very important people in the Egyptian hierarchy. Many of them had to live in the king's palace. Anytime the pharaoh or any of his viziers needed to dictate letters, edicts, or other state documents, the scribes were the one to write such documents."

"So everything either the pharaoh or vizier wanted to promulgate or to be in many copies had to be done by handwriting?"

"Yes, at the time of the pharaohs, there were no printing machines. Every document had to be written on papyrus. The instruments used by the scribes were very similar to those used for centuries afterward. Look at the picture showing the scribes' instruments—papyrus as paper, ink made of plant tint dur-

THIS IS HOW A SCRIBE LOOKED LIKE

ing this time, and a pen made of wood sharpened at the end. Voilà, as you say in French."

"Whoa! You speak French too?"

"No, I don't. I used these few words just to impress you. Now that you know who the people that lived in the pharaoh's palace were, I can tell you about me living there as a kid. Let me describe how people's everyday lives were. Naturally, I will start with my own life as the son of the pharaoh and his heir."

"Go ahead. Tell me."

Every morning, as the sun rose, my mom would come and wake me up with

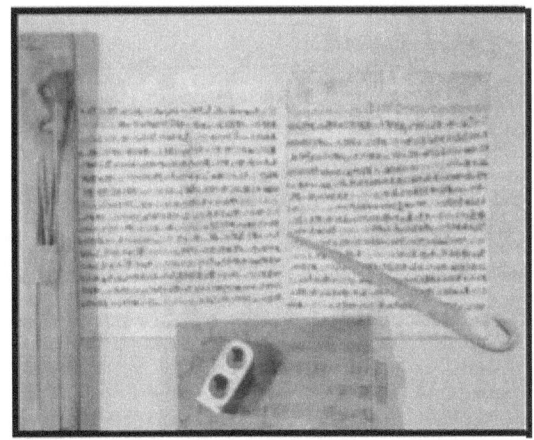

PAPYRUS WAS A PLANT THAT COULD BE PROCESSED TO BE USED AS PAPER. THIS PICTURE SHOES A SHEET OF PAPYRUS ,A PEN AND A SMALL POT OF INK

a sweet kiss on my forehead, as it was the custom in my family. This was one of the only times of the day when I would enjoy being with my mom alone. Then a couple of servants—they were like nannies to me—would come and take me to the bathroom and prepare a nice bath for me. There I would get in a tub that was filled with warm soapy water, and I would be rubbed and washed till the two nannies felt I was clean enough in their opinion. They used natron as soap. I know you will ask me what natron is."

"So what is a natron soap?"

"Well, Kendall, natron is an Egyptian product used by the pharaoh's family and by the very rich and famous Egyptians of this time. It is like a wet sodium carbonate. I don't know if this explanation satisfies you, but that is what it is. Every important person living in the palace, from the pharaoh to the viziers to the generals and others, had the privilege to use natron soap. You may find this disgusting today, but then it was a top-of-the-line product used by the privileged.

"Well, my nannies kept scrubbing and scrubbing me with this stuff, and honestly, I still could not understand why they always thought I needed more cleaning. But apparently, according to the custom of my country, being clean was not only about having a clean body. The bath was also supposed to clean my soul of all bad spirits that may have found their way during my sleep. As crazy as it sounds, that was the belief of this time."

"Then?"

"Then they dressed me up, and I was ready to go and have breakfast with my mom. That took place under the supervision of the nobleman in charge of my education.

When he decided that I was clean and properly dressed, he would lead me to have breakfast with my mom and dad in a private breakfast room.

THAT IS WHAT A MODERN SALUKI DOG LOOKS LIKE

"After finishing breakfast, I would be led to the quarters where I was schooled. There I had to join the other sons and daughters of the pharaoh for some courses, like the use of hieroglyphs, grammar, composition, math, and legal language."

"Then?"

"Then, as the heir of the throne, some courses were to be given to me alone. These included the pharaoh's heaven education, music of the gods, juggling with and controlling cobra snakes, sorcerer's magic, and chariot riding. Yes, that was part of what I had to know as the future pharaoh."

"Did you ever had a chance to play?"

"Yes. In the midmorning, I had a break from my studies. During this break, I went in the two large courtyards between the small rooms where classes were held. There I could play with my dog. His name was Saluki. And that curiously became, with time, the name of this race of dogs. This Egyptian dog is famous for not being able to bark. I have a picture of my dog for you to see."

"Who did you play with?"

"I was socializing and playing between classes with my half-brothers and sisters. I had two favorite friends, a boy and a girl. Jon-Jon Tee, although not a prince, was really as close to me as a brother, and my girlfriend was Mange Ta Soupe. I called her Mangie. Jon-Jon was adopted by one of the important priests of the palace. He was an apprentice sorcerer and was trained by this priest to become a sorcerer."

"I did not know that you had to learn to be a sorcerer. And how's that?"

"Apparently, yes, you have to learn to be a sorcerer. How that is, I don't know."

"Well, that is interesting."

"As such, he often played tricks that amused us very much. Mangie was very pretty, just as you are, Kendall. She looked very much like you and had pretty much the same manners as you have. That is why I believe that you are a princess of royal blood as she was. She was the daughter of a royal princess who was one of my mom's best friends. We used to often play together, and she and her mom had very often breakfasted with my mom and I when my dad could not join us. I will tell you more about them in a moment."

"OK, I will wait."

"Jon-Jon was a very special person. Being an apprentice sorcerer, he needed only air to live. He would eat and drink for pleasure, but he did not need to do so to survive. Like any sorcerer, he was incapable of sleep. Like any sorcerer, he could not get sick, but he may die like a human from an accident or in a war. Sorcerers are different from human beings as they can live for as long as five hundred years. The first two hundred years, they are apprentices. They look like people. In this case, Jon-Jon looked like he was the same age as I was. That was by the sorcerer's plan."

"So Jon-Jon was made to look like he was the same age as you were. Who did that?"

"The priest who trained him to become a sorcerer."

"Oh! OK, it's very strange for me to believe."

"As a sorcerer, he had white eyelashes. All sorcerers, male or female, had white eyelashes. Enough said about Jon-Jon being a sorcerer, although there is so much more to know about him. He loved to do magic with us—me and Mangie. One time, to impress us, he created a dark room by a twist of the finger. As we looked inside it, Mangie and I, it was full of black spiders crawling all around. By a twist of his finger again, they all seemed to direct themselves by the hundreds toward us. Mangie and I screamed and ran away as Jon-Jon was laughing his head off. Again, by a twist of his finger, the whole room and the spiders disappeared."

"I don't think I would appreciate that."

"If we felt like playing with a ball and none was around, again he would twist his fingers, and there a ball appeared at our feet. Sometimes his magic and tricks were scary, and sometimes they were amusing.

"Mangie and I were always looking for each other after each class when we were allowed to go to the recreation court between classes. We would share confidences and secrets, and we would tell each other nice jokes and stories. She was always very impressed by Jon-Jon's magic tricks and would try again and again to make them happen, always without success. And that frustrated her, as she believed that anything a boy could do, a girl could do

PICTURE SHOWING A PRINCE HUNTING
DURING THE PHARAONIC TIME.

better."

"Yes, indeed that was true then, and it is true now."

"Back to the palace, Kendall, and to what I had to do there on a daily basis. The large courtyard between the rooms where I had classes was also the place where I had to ride different horses, sometimes more than a couple of hours a day. This was always done between classes of math, language, and other subjects. Often it was a very important general of the armed forces of my father's army who taught me how to ride horses and trained me in the art of the war. Often, as part of my training, one of the generals would take me hunting or fishing with him and a group of very important people from my dad's palace."

"Did you like hunting and fishing? And if so, what did you like most?"

"I liked the two of them. The kind of hunting they took me to consisted of catching all kinds of large birds that we would bring to the palace for the cook to prepare for the next meal. We also caught fish by throwing some kind of spear with a thread attached to it. And if it hit the fish, it was ours. Well, that was a nice way to have fun, and my dad was often asking me how I was doing in my hunting and my fishing. That was pretty much my daily life as I was growing up without any worries as the pharaoh's son and heir.

"Sometimes, after my father completed his day's audiences, he would ask that I join him to pay tribute to the chief god, Amun-Ra. It was a pain for me to do so. But according to the traditions, if my father, the pharaoh, wouldn't do it, the empire could lose its divine order or *Maat*, and it could descend into *Isfet* (chaos), and my dad would be held responsible by the grand priest and by all the people for that.

"Accompanied by the high priest, my dad and I would walk through the great temple to the sanctuary, enjoying the cool air and smelling the thick incense. Inside we would approach the statue of Amun-Ra. My dad would ask the god some questions and receive answers from the high priest. Once the question session was over, my dad and I would be presented with a large bull. The picture you see here is part of the temple leading to the sanctuary."

"Nice picture."

"After prayers, the sacred butcher would cut the bull's throat as a sacrifice to the gods. Later, my dad would join my mom and me in the palace for some lunch. Afterward, I had to go back to school, and often my dad would jump into his royal chariot for a tour of the city. This was long before photography was invented, so few people knew what the pharaoh looked like. When he did that, crowds of Egyptians would gather in the streets to catch a sight of their divine ruler. Sometimes, in the late afternoon, I would join my dad in going to the temple for a ceremony marking the setting of the sun and the end of the day. After that, we would go back home for some time with my mom and for an early night.

"That was, my sweet friend Kendall, my everyday life in the pharaoh's palace."

4 The Ceremonial March to the Pharaoh's Audience Hall

"Hello again, my sweet Kendall. As I promised you before, when you will see me as of now, you will feel that you are dreaming. Oh no, no, no, no, I am not hypnotizing you—not at all. In these dreams, you will feel and visualize my experience as the small boy I was when I was growing up in the pharaoh's palace. You should know me not only as the pharaoh's son but also as the prince—a very special prince and the heir to the pharaoh's throne."

"OK."

"One Friday morning, as I was sound asleep, I woke up hearing a loving voice tell me, 'Come on. Get up, lazy bum. It is already six o'clock in the morning, and you are still asleep, Khouf.'

"That was my dad, the pharaoh, talking to me.

"It was not the habit for a pharaoh to wake his children up in the palace. However, my dad, who was a very loving person, decided this morning to do so.

"'Oh my god!' I said. 'It is this Friday.'

"This was the day my dad promised me that I would join him in the audience hall of the palace. The audience hall of the palace was a large hall where the pharaoh kept court. I started to quickly get dressed by myself using my everyday kind of dress.

"And as I was getting dressed, my mom and several servants entered the room. My mom told the servant, 'Today Khouf shall not get dressed as he does every day. Today he should wear the formal dress that the son of the pharaoh and the heir of the throne should wear when attending an official ceremony.' The servants came around me, holding all kinds of clothing. I looked at them as

they took out all that I would be wearing, and I thought I was dreaming and was in a fairy tale.

"They told me as they took away my clothes that I had to take a bath first. Well, I said that I took a bath every day. They handed me a special soap and told me that I should use this soap only for very special occasions, and this was a special occasion. I soaped and bathed myself. And when I finished my bath and dried myself, they rubbed my body with a special oil. This oil was lightly perfumed. 'Oh wow,' I said, 'I like this smell.' The servants told me that this perfume was used to please the gods protecting me. When I was nicely dried and perfumed, they made me wear a wrapped skirt of gold-and-blue linen. It felt so good. It was soft on the skin and was so pretty. They then placed around my neck what looked like a large round bib decorated with gold, blue, and red flower motifs. They then placed bracelets around my arms as well as around my wrists. They placed a wide gold-and-green scarf on me. After combing my hair with some sticky stuff, they placed an elongated bonnet with the gold head of a snake in front of it and an elaborately designed flat green crown.

This crown looked like spirals with balls on top of it. Then they made me wear a pair of golden sandals. Oh, Kendall! I liked those sandals, and they fit me very well.

"When I was all dressed up, my mother looked at me and analyzed every garment I was wearing. She approved the way I looked and said, 'This is the way the son of the pharaoh should be dressed for the circumstance.'

"My mother then took me aside, sat me in a chair, as you see in the picture of my mother and me, and started to explain to me, telling me, 'You are dressed this way for the very special ceremony that will take place today. You know your dad as the wonderful and loving dad he is to you.'

"'Yes, I know.'

"'Till now, that is the only way you know him. But your dad is also the king of Egypt. He was chosen by the gods to be the pharaoh, even before he was born. The gods decided that he would be their representative on earth and therefore made him a living god for all the Egyptian population.'

"This may not make sense to you today, Kendall, but this was the belief of every single Egyptian of that time. I mean, all the people had to live by the pharaoh's (the living god's) rule. Anyway, Kendall, I will get back to my talk with my mother that day.

"My mother took my two hands in hers, looked me in the eyes, and told me, 'Darling Khouf, till today, you grew up living in the private quarters of the pharaoh. These quarters consisted of our home and the pharaoh's private apartment, as well as of his other wives' quarters. Next to our quarters are the private school and court for you and

73

your half-brothers and sisters, as well as the quarters for the servants assigned to all of us. All these quarters are a very small part of the palace. Your dad's palace is much, much larger.'

"Remember, Kendall, that I described to you earlier in the previous talk that the palace where I was living in was built by my granduncle, Amenophis III.

"'Khouf,' my mother said, 'soon a chamberlain of the pharaoh, followed by a delegation of other noblemen, will come to guide you through the palace to the large audience hall where the pharaoh, your father, will be presiding. There will be hundreds of officials—a whole hierarchy of people whose job it is to govern as instructed by your dad.'

"'Mother,' I said, 'what is a chamberlain? Also, what does an hierarchy of people mean?'

"'Darling,' said my mom, 'a chamberlain is a nobleman who is also a chief officer in the household of the pharaoh and who often introduces people either to the pharaoh or in the name of the pharaoh to the people who are in his audience.'

"'Thanks, Mom.'

"'Khouf, an hierarchy of people is a group of people organized in ranks in a way that each is subordinate to the one above him. In this case, it is a body of persons to whom your dad, the pharaoh, gave authority to perform certain duties. First you have the viziers, who get their orders directly from the pharaoh. These people will be sitting in the audience hall just under where you and your dad will be sitting. One vizier oversees the treasury, another will be responsible for the granary, and others will have similar responsibilities. Then you will see also other people who form the government of the pharaoh, such as town mayors, scribes, doorkeepers, and much more.'

"'Thanks, Mom,' I said.

"Just as a way of comparison to you, Kendall, you could say that my father was like your president. The viziers of the pharaoh will be like the president's Cabinet secretaries. And like in your country's government, each secretary will be the head of a department. Each government's department has many employees working there, several thousands in some of them. These people are grouped in different offices, and each office has several divisions."

"Thanks, Khouf. This is very interesting."

"Well, let me get back to what my mom said to me about my dad's government. She said, 'Khouf, the audience hall will be full of people, and all of them will be looking up at you as this is the first audience you attend, and they want to know more of the young man that would one day be their king, their god, and their boss. So, darling, no need for me to tell you that you have to conduct yourself with dignity and act in a very gracious way as the son of the pharaoh, their ruler.'

"'I get it, Mom,' I said.

"My mom then told me, 'When the chamberlain comes, he will invite

PICTURE SHOWING MY MOM LISTENING TO THE CHAMBERLAIN. MY MOM HOLDING THE EMBLEMS IDENTIFYING HER AS THE PHARAOHS WIFE, MOTHER OF THE HEIR TO THE THRONE OF EGYPT.

you to sit on a chair that will be carried by four men who will walk behind him, and he will guide you with pomp in a very ceremonial way through all the palace corridors where people working for your dad have their offices. This walk will end at the audience hall close to where your dad, the pharaoh, will be sitting. Once you are next to your dad, standing up in front of the chair where you will be sitting, he will introduce you to the whole audience there. They will all applaud you, and you will have to smile with grace and modesty. When your dad will ask you to sit down, you will sit and follow what will be said there. It will sound very boring to you at first, but you better get used to it as one day you will be the pharaoh, and you will be the one to make the decisions and give the orders. To be a prince or a princess sounds wonderful to many, but one of the duties of a prince or a princess is to attend ceremonies like this one, where you will be bored.'

"As my mother finished explaining those things to me, a servant entered the room and loudly announced, 'Chamberlain Barouf is here to escort His Royal Highness, the prince Khouf, to the audience.'

"My mother instructed the servant to invite the chamberlain in, and so he did. As soon as he was in, the chamberlain and four noblemen that accompanied him kneeled in front of my mother and me. My mother greeted them in our name and told them they could stand up now. My mother then addressed the chamberlain and told him, 'This is the first time that Prince Khouf will be attending the pharaoh's official audience.'

"The chamberlain promised my mother that he shall take good care of me, and he very respectfully asked me to follow him and accompany him. The chamberlain, the four noblemen, and I then went out of the court of the pharaoh's private apartment. There a group of people dressed in all kinds of uniforms was waiting for us. First there were six soldiers in parade uniform, each holding a decorated spear, and waiting in two rows for us. Then there were four cymbalists, each with a cymbal in each hand, striking them clankingly together. There were also two other musicians playing a pharaonic musical instrument known as the triangle with a metal beater. There was also a chaise at the center of all these people."

"A chaise, Khouf? You mean a chair."

"No, Kendall. A chaise, my sweet Kendal, is a one-person chair with four legs and a calash top. This chaise was a very special chaise. It was at the center of what looked like a miniature boat. This type of chaise was only to be used by the pharaoh, the heir to the throne of Egypt, the grand priest, and the statues of the gods of Egypt. The boat carrying the chaise had two long horizontal sticks, each alongside of it, so that four people could carry it. There were four noblemen, each on a corner of this miniature boat. They invited me to sit on the chaise, and the four noblemen raised the boat with the chaise where I was sitting and carried it.

"The four noblemen, who carried the boat where I sat, followed the four cymbalists and the two musicians. The chamberlain alone walked ahead of the noblemen carrying me. All the people surrounding me were placed as if there were there to protect me. Four servants, each with a feather fan at the end of a long stick, framed me. As the procession was advancing, these servants were fanning me. Then finally, walking behind my chaise were four other soldiers in parade uniform, each holding a decorated spear.

"As we were advancing, all the people around this procession were singing songs that were in my honor. The songs' words were saying, 'Here is the son of the pharaoh, our god on earth, the future pharaoh of Egypt. Bow your heads, kneel out of respect for the one who will be your king and master,' and all kinds of similar wording.

"Kendall, in our family quarters where I grew up, I was not used to this kind of stuff in my honor. These words were reserved for my dad, the pharaoh. Honestly, I felt a little funny and embarrassed for being the center of so much attention. In addition, all the stuff that I was wearing suffocated me. I was perspiring, and all I wanted was some fresh air and breeze.

"Kendall! My mind started to wander. I asked myself, 'Why so much fuss for me?' Ah, I thought that it was because I was a prince. I was the son of the pharaoh. So that's what it was to be a prince. To be the son of a king or a descendant of a king, or is it to be a member of a family who had some royal blood? Whatever it was, for me it meant to be seated in a chaise and displayed to people who were almost forced to bow for you, even if they did not give a hoot for who you were."

"So did you like that? Tell me the truth, as you kept telling me that I am a princess. If I go to Egypt now, would they do this kinds of things for me?"

"No, Kendall. I do not think so. But wow, what an ego boost I felt then—that is, if one had a big ego. And what a comedy this was for one that did not see why he or she would really deserve all that fuss. Then I started to think again. All this uproar, all this brouhaha, because a so-called prince was transported, almost like merchandise, held by four men from one point to another. I would have preferred to have walked from where I was to where I had to be. It was not really fun to be a prince or a princess for that matter. Too much was asked of you, and the reward—if that was to be considered as a reward—was to have all these people, ones who really didn't know you other than as the prince, hypocritically bow to you while thinking, Why should I do that for that idiot-looking person?

"Strangely, most young ladies, maybe you included, Kendall, like to see themselves as princesses. In your case, you probably are a descendant of a king, but you are lucky because where you live, and in today's world, they don't move you like merchandise in a chaise and have all kinds of people bow to you. Your mom and dad know that you are a princess, and in their eyes, like in any parents' eyes, their daughters are always princesses. So enjoy it as long as they don't sit you in a chaise and parade you around."

"Wow, what a story, Khouf."

"Well, yes it is. As I was being paraded in that silly chaise, all I was thinking of was my sweet friend Mangie. Remember, her real name is Mange Ta Soupe. I wanted her to be with me. I saw her in my mind as a princess, my sweet princess with whom I felt so good.

"Well, as I was daydreaming, this procession, music and all, created quite a commotion from the moment it started. This commotion attracted the attention of the pharaoh's wives and other children in the pharaoh's quarters. Almost immediately, the private court between the rooms where my mom and I lived and the harem's rooms, where all the other pharaoh's wives and their children lived, filled with the other pharaoh's children and their moms. Most of them, including my friends Jon-Jon and Mangie, were just curious as they never saw such a formal procession. And soon, seeing me sitting in that chaise with all the honors that surrounded me, they realized that this procession was around me and about me. As the procession approached my friends Jon-Jon and Mangie, I greeted them, shouting, 'Hello, Jon-Jon! Hello, Mangie!'

"I was immediately reminded by the noblemen that in my role as the prince, being carried ceremoniously as I was, I should not address any one of those looking at my procession. The pharaoh's wives and all the children of the pharaoh's quarters were talking to one another, pointing their fingers toward the procession, and most of them were waving their hands and applauding us in a friendly way. All these women—the mothers of the pharaoh's children, the concubines, and the other relatives of the pharaoh—were singing and shouting, 'Hallelujah, hallelujah. Here is the eldest son of our pharaoh and of our living god, and our future pharaoh. We wish a long life to our future pharaoh.'

"As these children and women applauded and sang, a woman and a child were looking at the procession with envy and disgust. This woman was the Syrian princess that my father, the pharaoh, married. Remember, Kendall, I told you that my dad married this woman as a political gesture to the vanquished Syrian king to gain his alliance. As I also told you, almost everyone was sure that my dad did not sire her son, as at that time he was conducting a war far away from home. But my dad, in a magnanimous gesture, decided not to fuss about it, considered the boy as his own, and named him Syroman.

"Well, this boy and his mother, instead of joining the crowd in waving, applauding, and rejoicing, were shouting insults and words of envy. The mother, suddenly realizing how crazy it was to do so, stopped shouting insults and tried to keep her son quiet, promising him that he would be the pharaoh and not me after the death of my dad. Saying that caused a great scandal among the women that surrounded her. Twistmind, the priest with a twisted mind that befriended the Syrian princess and who became my tutor after my dad's death, came to her rescue before the other women could accuse her of treason and beat her for what she and her son just said.

"He used his sorcery's power. In just a moment, using some magic words and gestures, he rubbed his nose three times with two fingers of his left hand, and then he looked at these women directly in their eyes and hypnotized them all. And he made all of them forget what was just said by the Syrian princess and her son. He then turned to the Syrian princess and told her, 'Are you out of your mind to say something like that? This is an act of high treason for which you may lose your life. Yes, at the right time I will make things happen. Remember, this is not only your son, as the two of us know. But till then, secrecy must be our way.'

"As incredible as that can be, I overheard this conversation and witnessed the magic of this wicked man hypnotizing all these women. I did not know then that when my dad would die, this man would become my tutor, and that as a tutor, he would betray me, as well as his country and much more as I will tell you later, my sweet Kendall. Despite all the glamour that surrounded me then, I felt so uncomfortable with what this man said. And I had a premonition that this man was trouble—trouble for me and trouble for his country as you will see later.

"As a young boy, I soon became wrapped up in what was surrounding me—the soldiers in parade uniform with their spears, the cymbalists, the musicians playing, and the noblemen carrying my chaise. I felt like a prince. And yes, I just came to realize I was indeed one. This musical procession crossed the private area of the palace—the area where I was raised and where my mom and all the other princesses and their servants lived. Now the procession left this area and entered the very long corridor separating the area of the palace where the pharaoh and his family lived from the area where the palace's top officials had their offices.

"We were advancing in this corridor toward the large audience hall at the other extremity of the palace. The procession proceeded in this area where the officials had their offices. Who were these officials? And why were they called the officials? I already told you that the officials were the people that were responsible administering the country in the name of the pharaoh. The doorkeepers and several other functions were also considered as official functions, and I will describe that to you later. For now, the procession was just crossing the area where these officials had their offices. It was directing itself slowly toward the large audience hall at the other end of this corridor.

"At times, Kendall, I could hardly force myself not to laugh, seeing all these people bowing and kneeling as the chamberlain was announcing my passage through these areas. I kept pinching myself not to laugh loudly, and I kept waving my hands here and there to all these people kneeling as they saw the procession approaching them. 'Wow,' I kept telling myself as I was nicely sitting in that chaise, being carried by these noblemen. 'Wow, I did not know that I was such an important person to these people.' Then again, I would tell myself I must be, but if I was so important, that did not mean that my mom would not punish me if I misbehaved or that my dad, the pharaoh, would not reprimand me if I did not get good grades from my teachers.

"We finally arrived in front of a small room adjacent to the pharaoh's large audience room. There the procession stopped. The musicians stopped playing their instruments. The cymbalists stopped striking their cymbals, and the singing stopped too. There was absolute silence, and suddenly everyone around me became very quiet. Then I was invited by the chamberlain to leave my chair. I was helped getting out of it by the noblemen, and I was led to the small room next to the pharaoh's audience. There the chamberlain offered me a seat and sat next to me. Everyone else in my procession remained outside of this room and were either standing up or kneeling, depending on their hierarchic position.

"As we were alone in this room, the chamberlain told me, 'Your dad instructed me to let you know and to explain to you all that is about to happen. He told me that he would have an exceptional audience with all the officials of his administration.'

"'Thank you, sir.'

"'First, as your dad will enter the great hall, everyone in the audience will kneel and say, "Long live the pharaoh." Then at the invitation of the pharaoh, they will stand

FICTURE OF AN OLD EGYPTIAN TEMPLE IN UFPER EGYPT. NOTICE HOW BEAUTIFUL IS THE CEILING AND THE CAPITALS OF THE COLUMNS

up, and depending on their ranks, some will be invited to sit down, and the others will either stand up or will remain kneeling. The pharaoh will then ask one of his chamberlains to invite you into the audience hall. Once you will be there, he will start this audience by formally introducing you to all the officials of his administration.'

"As the chamberlain kept talking, Kendall, what he was saying started to sound like so much bla bla bla, and somehow I got bored. I discovered that the door leading from the room where we were and the pharaoh's large audience hall was slightly open. I glanced through the crack at what was inside this room. My eyes were curiously looking inside the audience hall, and wow, what was I seeing there.

"The chamberlain continued talking, telling me that I would be introduced as the pharaoh's heir and as the heir to the throne of Egypt. As he will do so, everyone in the audience—yes, everyone—will kneel and say, 'Long live the pharaoh, our king and god. And long live his son and the heir to the throne of Egypt.' As they do that, Kendall, I will have to stand up and bow to my dad and also say, 'Long live the pharaoh, our king and god.'

"The audience hall was a large and very beautiful room. It had two rows of columns. Each of the columns had a large diameter. It was so large that it took about four men holding hands to go around its circumference. Each column was crowned with a capital having the shape of a lotus flower. The lotus flower is a water lily. Its shape was used in our architecture to crown the columns.

"To help you imagine how immense these columns are, look, I chose this recent picture of an old Egyptian temple where this type of column was used. Look at the size of the people at the base of the columns and how small they looked compared to the columns. Also, look how beautiful the design was of the column capital.

"The columns and all the walls of the audience hall were all carved with scenes of the pharaoh and the gods of Egypt. The walls and columns of the following picture are very similar to the walls and columns of the palace audience hall. As you can see, part of the back wall shows a picture of a pharaoh with a bird-god's head, return-ing victorious after having vanquished

VIEW SHOWING WHAT THE PALACE LARGE AUDIENCE HALL'S WALLS AND COLUMNS WOULD LOOK LIKE

Egypt's enemies. The front wall is divided in four parts horizontally, three of which are obvious. The lower part consists of lotus flower decorations. The central part of the wall shows the pharaoh facing different gods and paying his respect to them. The third horizontal row shows two scenes of the pharaoh on his chariot, returning from either a hunting trip or from war. All the scenes were colored in brilliant colors and were surrounded with inscriptions telling the stories of the events represented. It was breathtaking to see what was done with this room.

"As I kept marveling in my mind on what I was watching, the chamberlain kept talking and explaining to me more about the glorious history of my country. Yes, Kendall, my beautiful Egyptian princess, this is also the country of your dad's ancestors."

"You know, Khouf, I never looked at that—I mean, the glorious history of Egypt the way you are describing it to me. Tell me more."

"I will tell you first how Egypt became a country, as told to me by the chamberlain, and how the Egypt of the pharaohs became the most powerful country in the world for more than three thousand years. First you should know that Egypt owed its existence as a country and its civilization to the river Nile. Without the river Nile crossing the land of Egypt, at its center from south to north, the area where Egypt is would have been just a desert. You can see that very clearly in the map shown here for you. The river Nile is the longest river in the world. It flows from Lake Victoria, in the country now known as Uganda, all the way to the Mediterranean Sea in the north of Egypt."

"I knew that Egypt was crossed by the Nile, but I did not know that this river was the longest river in the world. That is news to me."

"For a long time, the Egyptians as well as all the people living alongside the river Nile believed that the river was a god. Every year, during the rainy season, the Nile would be filled with rain-water flowing from Lake Victoria and from the areas around this lake in Uganda, as well as from areas that are known today as Sudan and Ethiopia. These countries are located in Central Africa."

"I did not know that the Nile crossed all these countries from Central

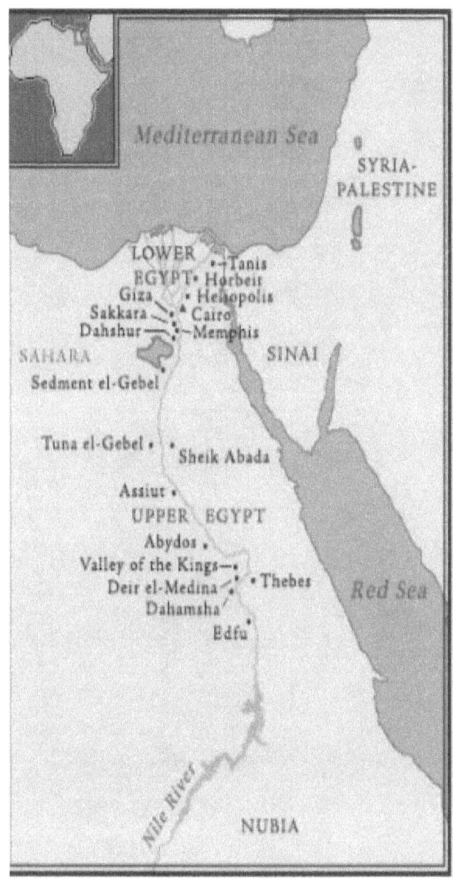

Africa to Egypt and then to the sea. So they all depended on this river for their survival."

"Yes, indeed. The Nile's branches that start in these countries are known as the White Nile and the Blue Nile. These two branches generate lots of additional water. They all connect somewhere in what is Sudan today, and from there flow toward Egypt. Once the Nile enters Egypt, it will be so full of water that it will overflow its banks and inundate a large portion of land alongside its border."

"Wow, keep talking, Khouf. You know so much."

Fernand W. Dahan

PICTURE SHOWING AN EGYPTIAN PRIEST

"The Nile did not only bring water to Egypt but also brought with it a kind of silt that can be described as a combination of topsoil and fertilizer. Every year, in the month of October, the floodwater would recede and would leave the silt that came with the water right there in the soil. That rendered this soil exceptionally fertile.

"Because of that, very soon in the history of mankind, Egyptians started to cultivate the land to produce food to eat. You will understand, therefore, that the majority of the people who lived in Egypt at the time when my dad was the pharaoh were peasant farmers. I would say to you that nine out of ten people were farmers."

"So most of the Egyptians were farmers. Wow."

"With the Nile being a god, Egyptian priests were making all kinds of offering to it. I will tell you more on this subject in a moment, OK?"

"Yes. OK."

"Many farmers were working in their own small lots. Others were hired to work on the land of the pharaoh or on the land owned by the temples' priests. Another group of peasants worked on the land of the few very rich people that were given land by the pharaoh. These people were either great generals or people that helped the pharaoh, and they were considered noble. So every year in the month of October, when the floodwater would recede, everyone—farmers and owners—would mark out the boundaries of their lots. They would also clear and repair the irrigation channels, and the farmers would be plant their crops."

"If I understand you well, most of the farmers were working for others, and these others were rich and powerful."

PICTURE SHOWING EGYPTIAN FARMERS AT WORK

"Yes, you get the picture correctly. Some years, when it did not rain so much in Central Africa, very little water would flow in the Nile toward Egypt, and many of the areas that were flooded would not be irrigated, and therefore no silt would be deposited to allow the farmers to cultivate the land and produce food to eat. That would be catastrophic for Egypt. Remember the story in the Bible when Joseph interpreted the dream of the pharaoh? He predicted seven years of an abundant crop followed by seven years of famine, as no food could be produced from cultivating the land."

"Keep talking. This is so interesting."

"Most of the Egyptians of this time believed that if they did not please the god Nile, then the god Nile would not generate enough water to cultivate the land and pro-

duce food. Therefore, every year, in order to please the god Nile, they would give the Nile a bride. They would choose the prettiest farm girl as a maiden for the god Nile, dress her as a bride, and cover her with all kinds of beautiful jewels. Then in an official ceremony, with all the government people and the powerful people of the time attending, they would throw her alive into the Nile, where she would drown."

"That was terrible and very cruel."

"Yes, indeed that was a most terrible and cruel thing to do. Throwing a pretty farm girl alive every year in the Nile became a ritual—a very cruel ritual. But they kept doing it, convinced that by doing so, the Nile would bring its water and silt and would fertilize the land.

"After quite a few years of this cruel ritual, handsome young men, all of whom were sons of government officials and of the powerful, began to disappear. Most of the time, their disappearance occurred when they would go to or be near the Nile River. Many people claimed to have seen at nightfall beautiful mermaids rising from the river and tempting these young men to join them.

"Somehow, after that, the men would disappear and would never be heard from. According to the legend, the numerous women that were sacrificed and drowned in the Nile River revived and became mermaids. These were then named nilemaids. They formed an underwater kingdom, or as it became known then, a queendom. In an act

of revenge over the powerful of the time, they kidnapped the young men and submitted them to slavery under the water. After quite a few years of these disappearances and the realization that sacrificing these women was costing them the lives of their young men, the rich and powerful convinced the pharaoh to replace the pretty live women sacrificed to the Nile River with pretty dolls dressed as brides.

"Since that time, the nilemaids that were the mermaids of the Nile River ceased to attract the young men of the rich and powerful into drowning in river, except when a rich or powerful man would do real harm to a young woman. Then the nilemaids would avenge this woman by attracting and drowning the son of this person."

"Good, I like that. So Egyptian nilemaids were the beginning of women's lib. Great, it started in Egypt. More power to the nilemaids."

"So goes the legend according to what the chamberlain was telling me. Let's get back to crops that the farmers were planting when the Nile River water would recede, leaving the silt there. The two main crops that were planted were wheat and barley. They would make bread with

the wheat, and they would make beer with the barley. Yes, Kendall, the ancient Egyptians used to have lots of beer when my dad was the pharaoh. Unfortunately, lots of people would get drunk drinking too much beer. The farmers also planted in their small gardens vegetables such as lettuce and lentils. The large farms, those owned by the priests and the nobles, would have vineyards and would produce wine.

"Also, all small and big farmers would have cattle and poultry to supply their diet with meat. As you see, sweet princess, the ancient Egyptians ate pretty much like you do today here in your country. We did not have processed food then, and everything that was cooked was immediately consumed, as refrigerators were not yet invented.

"Lots of farmers also planted flax. The ancient Egyptians used flax to make linen. Most of the clothes at the time of the pharaohs were made out of linen.

"As the chamberlain finished telling me all that I am telling you, we felt lots of movement in the audience hall and heard the people shouting words of praise to my dad, the pharaoh. All this commotion indicated to us in the waiting room that the pharaoh was arriving or had arrived in the audience hall. A short time after that, the audience hall became very quiet, and one of the pharaoh's chamberlains widely opened the door separating the room where we were and the audience room and invited me to join my dad, the pharaoh."

"This must have been quite an experience for you as a young boy, not yet a man."

"Yes, Kendall, my experience with the first audience I attended there with my dad was overwhelming and so different from the experience I just shared with you. I will share it with you in detail in our next encounter."

"Good night, Khouf. I am so sleepy."

"Good night, sweet Kendall, and sweet dreams. You should never forget that you are a princess of royal Egyptian blood, and most of all, a princess for your mom, dad, and all those who love you so much. Sweet dreams, darling, and see you soon."

5 The Audience Hall Meeting and the Story of the General

"Hello again, Kendall. How was your day, princess?"

"It was fine, thank you. I thought a lot about what you told me about Egypt and the Egyptian farmers. And although what the nilemaids did took place thousands of years ago, they were really great."

"I'll take you from where I left last night. I have to give you long descriptions of what I saw, so please listen and see what I want to show you, OK?"

"OK."

"There I was at the door of the audience hall, facing the entire assembly. There was a raised platform where my dad, the pharaoh, was sitting in his throne. Next to my father's throne was an empty fancy chair, and on each of the two sides of them were two other chairs. Facing the platform was a large number of people filling the audience hall. In the first two rows were the viziers, and at their center was the grand vizier, the army officers, and other very high members of the pharaoh's government. All the remaining rows were filled with other government people standing up. A large empty aisle was at the center of the audience hall. The front wall was divided in four parts horizontally, three of which were obvious. The lower part consisted of lotus flower decorations, and the central part of the wall showed the pharaoh facing different gods and paying his respects to them.

"The chamberlain preceded me on the platform and invited me to follow him as he directed himself toward my dad. He soon reached a location facing the pharaoh. He kneeled and, in a firm and proud voice, said, 'Your Majesty, may you live, prosper, and be healthy. I have the distinct honor and privilege to have led to this hall and to Your Majesty, may you live, prosper, and be healthy, His Royal Highness, Prince Khouf, your eldest son and the heir to the throne of Egypt, after a long and fruitful life.'

"The pharaoh thanked the chamberlain and told him to sit on the chair on my right. Then he addressed the people in the audience hall. I was introduced again, this time by my dad, to the audience. He reiterated what the chamberlain said and added that the people of Egypt should know that I will be the next pharaoh after he passes away. He then invited me to sit in the fancy chair next to him. He then invited the grand vizier to join him on the platform and invited him to sit in one of the chairs next to his throne. The grand vizier sat as instructed by my dad. Then my dad turned to him again and asked him to read the meeting agenda. He stood up and kneeled, facing the pharaoh. And when instructed by the pharaoh, he stood up and ceremoniously read the meeting agenda.

"To make a long story short, the agenda consisted of two important parts. The first part dealt with reports from the different viziers on the state of the different ministries of the country, and the second part dealt almost completely with the return of General Vas Nu Pieds from a victorious battle he had with the Nubian people, whose country was located in the south of Egypt. After listening to the reading of the agenda, the pharaoh invited each vizier to report on the state of his ministry.

"That started the most boring part of the meeting for me. Honestly, I was not too interested about the details of what they talked about. So I started to get drowsy, almost falling asleep. Suddenly, I was briskly awakened by what seemed to be a weight over my knees. I opened my eyes and could not believe what I saw. Here, standing up on my lap, was a reduced sized of my grandmother. My grandmother passed away two years earlier and was buried with Grandpa like any member of the pharaoh's family. When she lived, she was normally tall like any other woman of my country. But here she was, on my lap, hardly two feet tall. Yes, almost as if she were a doll or maybe a little two-year-old girl. She looked me in the eyes and told me, 'Shame on you, Khouf. One day, all this information would be of the utmost importance when you accede to the throne of Egypt.'

"'Nana,' I said. That was the way I used to call my grandmother. 'Nana, I did not mean to do so, but I could not help but get bored with all this information that I really don't understand.'

"'I know, I know, Khouf. I came back for a reason. The reason I am here with you today is to talk to you about General Vas Nu Pieds. He has a long story, and his story is inspirational. The second part of this meeting will be to honor him. Here is his story:

PICTURE OF WHAT AN EGYPTIAN FARM LOOKED LIKE INCLUDING ON THE BACKGROUN FARMER'S LODGING

Vas Nu Pieds was a poor ignorant peasant working for a rich merchant who owned a large farm. He had many people working in his farm and produced all kinds of agricultural plants that he sold in the market and that made him a wealthy man. He was a good man and tried to be just with the people working for him.

"The picture that I am showing here," said Khouf to Kendall, is similar to the rich merchant's farm and to the lodging that he provided for these men and women."

This merchant was married to a young woman much younger than him. This woman was famous for her beauty and for being very coquettish. She would often go around the farm and look at the people working for her husband, often with disdain, and she made remarks that were not always appreciated by the workers. These workers could do nothing, however, as she was the boss's wife. One day, as she was going around the farm, she noticed Vas Nu Pieds. As I told you earlier, Vas Nu Pieds was poor and ignorant, but he was also very good-looking and he managed to be known by his fellow workers as a hardworking, honest, virtuous, and very pious man. For a couple of days after noticing him, she kept going around him, acting in a very coquettish way. The poor fellow first did not pay too much attention to what she was doing, but soon it became obvious to him that somehow she was after him.

He continued to act as if he did not notice her advances. He concentrated on his work and worked harder and harder. Realizing that he avoided paying attention to her, she approached him directly and told him, "Young man, you are really good-looking. Come with me and let us have fun together in bed."

He was so shocked when he realized what she was saying. He remained silent with his head bowed down. But when she insisted, he raised his head and very modestly, almost whispering, told her, "Madam, you are my boss's wife, and I am a poor ignorant worker. I have no business doing what you are asking me to do. That will make me betray my master on one hand and my principles on the other. Sorry, madam, I am an honest man, and as your humble servant and the humble servant of your husband, I could not and would not oblige. No, madam, I could not and would not do that."

Not accustomed to having her wishes—or maybe what she considered her orders—being refused, she got furious, and forgetting the difference of ranks between her and this poor peasant, she got uncontrollably angry and threatened him loudly for being ungrateful and evil. And she told him, "Look, boy! If you do not comply with my orders—and these orders are that you come with me and have fun with me in bed—I will accuse you of trying to rape me and have you punished by my husband accordingly."

The punishment for a lower-class person raping or attempting to rape an upper-class woman or a woman of any social class was death, with eternal banishment from life after death. Death was not so much of a punishment as being eternally banished from life after death for an honest and religious person of this time. Before she made up her mind of either trying one more time with Vas Nu Pieds or accusing him of attempting to rape her, Vas Nu Pieds, who was till then kneeling in front of her, as was the custom for a low-class peasant, stood up and ran away from her and from the farm where he was working. On the way out of the farm, he bumped into his mother and told her what happened with the wife of his master. His mother, who knew the consequences of such an accusation, could not do anything but approve of his running out of there, and she wished him good luck. Then she started to cry and lament for what was happening to her son.'

"Here my grandmother stopped talking. She took a deep breath and asked me if it would be all right for her to sit on my lap. Suddenly coming out of my torpor, I became conscious that I was there sitting in the pharaoh's audience hall with my father sitting in his throne next to me and all these people in the hall around us, watching us.

"Oh god, I felt they were watching me with that miniature woman standing on my lap. My grandma, realizing my being ill at ease, started to laugh loudly, adding to my embarrassment. She then said to me, 'Don't worry, Khouf. You are the only person here to see me and to hear me, and I am here to make sure you know the story of the wonderful man that Vas Nu Pieds is before he enters this audience hall. Now, darling, would you let me sit on your lap instead of remaining standing up? I am starting to feel very tired. Yes, Khouf, even a spirit like me can get tired of standing up that long, particularly as it is not that comfortable to be standing on top of someone's lap.'

"'Oh sure, Grandmother,' I replied, being reassured that I was the only one to see and hear her. So she sat down on my lap.

Vas Nu Pieds ran away from the farm, and for three days and two nights, he kept running and walking without any rest. Finally exhausted, he lay down under a tree in what looked like a small wood or forest on the Nile shore, and he fell asleep. When he woke up, hungry and a little lost as to where he was, he saw an old man with lots of hair, a beard, and heavy eyebrows sitting next to him and looking at him with compassion.

"Who are you?" Vas Nu Pieds asked. "And what am I doing here?"

"For you to know who I am now is not that important. Let me say that for you, I am a friend. You collapsed under this tree two days ago and kept sleeping since then."

The man's mannerism and choice of words indicated that he was from one of the upper class of Egyptian society, maybe a prince or a priest. This was strange, as the custom of the time was that men of this social class shaved their heads and their beards, as well as their eyebrows. It was much more important if such man was from the upper class or if he was from the priests' community.

"You must be very hungry, young man. Are you?"

"Oh yes, I am. That makes it maybe a week that I was without any food."

"Poor kid," the old man said. "I'll go and fish for you this time, but afterward, you will have to do so yourself."

And as he said so, he left Vas Nu Pieds, and using a tool that looked like a spear, he went to the river shore and in a moment caught a large fish, then again another one. The old man cleaned the fish, built a small fire, and rapidly roasted the two fish.

When they finished eating, with Vas Nu Pieds back to normal, if one can say that, he asked the old man, "Who are you, sir? And why are you so nice to me?"

"You can call me River Man, or better yet, Old

Man River. I was a priest in the temple of Aton, the god of all gods. When the pharaoh Akhnaton passed away many, many years ago, the grand priest of the Karnak temple took over the country and controlled the pharaoh, who was then a very young man with no experience, and he banned the Aton cult and anything dealing with this religion. As I insisted on keeping my faith, contrary to the wish of the new religious power, I was given a choice either to renounce my faith of else."

"What was the else, sir?"

"Well, I did not renounce my faith and was banned from all temples and was condemned to wander alone in these woods, hunting and fishing for food. As I protested this harsh treatment, the grand priest of the Karnack temple called on a famous sorcerer who was living there and asked him to 'do his thing.' 'His thing' was a curse. And the curse made sure that I would remain for the rest of my life living in this forest among rags, the animals, and the birds. And if I ever shaved my head, my beard, and my eyebrows, I would suffer from a sickness that would cause great pain all over my body and would handicap me forever. When I came in the forest, I was well received by the animals, and soon they were talking to me in their languages. I was able to communicate with them in their language. As a result, I decided not to hunt for food and since then went fishing to nourish myself."

Vas Nu Pieds was very upset in realizing how wicked people could be and how revengeful they would be for matters that really should remain very personal.

"Vas Nu Pieds then told his story to Old Man River," said my grandmother. "And it will be needless for me to repeat it for you, Khouf, as you already know it."

"Now what are your plans?" said Old Man River.

"I really don't know. All I know is that I don't want to die, and I want to remain true to my beliefs."

"Well, well," said Old Man River. "Let's see what we can do. First, let's talk of survival. Next time, you will have to learn to fish with the means we have here—that is, with almost no tools other than the ones we will make with what we can find around here. No hunting in 'my forest' as all the animals here are friends, and we have a pact to defend one another from strangers. Then we will have to find a permanent solution for you, my young friend. One idea could be to join the army—the pharaoh's army. How would you like to do that?"

"What other choice do I have?" Asked Vas Nu Pieds.

"Well, you can stay here and join me in hermit life and risk to be found by your master's people and be brought back to the farm where only the gods know what they will do to you if they don't choose to kill you. Another choice is to continue to run, looking for better opportunities, and maybe, or maybe not, you will find one."

"This is a no-brainier," said Vas Nu Pieds. "What do I have to do to join the pharaoh's army? And how soon could that happen?"

"We have to develop a plan for you to join the army," Old Man River then suggested.

"Yes, I guess so," said Vas Nu Pieds.

"Every now and then, I see a group of young men recruited by the pharaoh's army recruiter. They go by here on their way to their training camp. They all seem to be happy-go-lucky. They sing and they laugh as they walk in small formations directed by one of the pharaoh's sergeants, and they are very friendly with people accosting them. So if you go and stand along their route, there is a good chance you can bump into them and ask them if you can join them and go and serve the pharaoh with them.'"

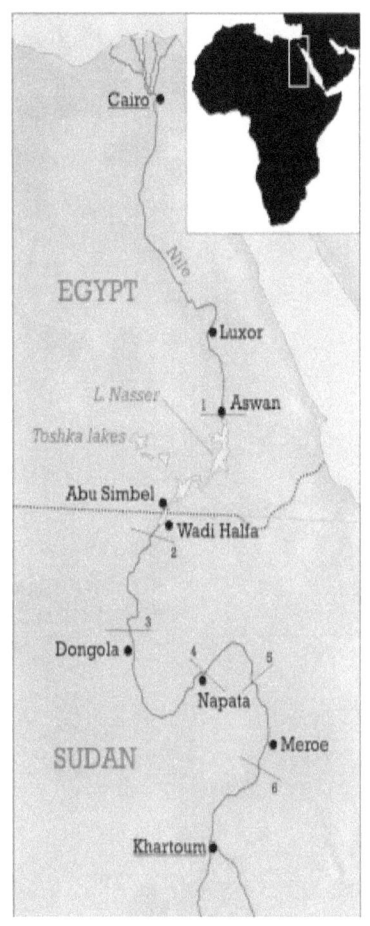

"My grandmother then said, 'Hey, Khouf, I am getting into too many details, and it is almost time for the next item of the agenda, so let me hurry up for you to be able to understand what will follow.'

"'OK, Grandmother.'

Vas Nu Pieds did as suggested by Old Man River and was welcomed to join the next singing group of recruits. These young men were directed to a training camp and were instructed in the art of making war, according to the Egyptian rules of war. Vas Nu Pieds was a fast learner, and despite the fact that he did not know how to read or write, he was soon ready for combat. The first expedition he was sent to was a war against the Nubian kingdom. The king of the Nubians wanted to appropriate himself some land in the south of Egypt and annex it to his kingdom. The modern map shown here, projected on

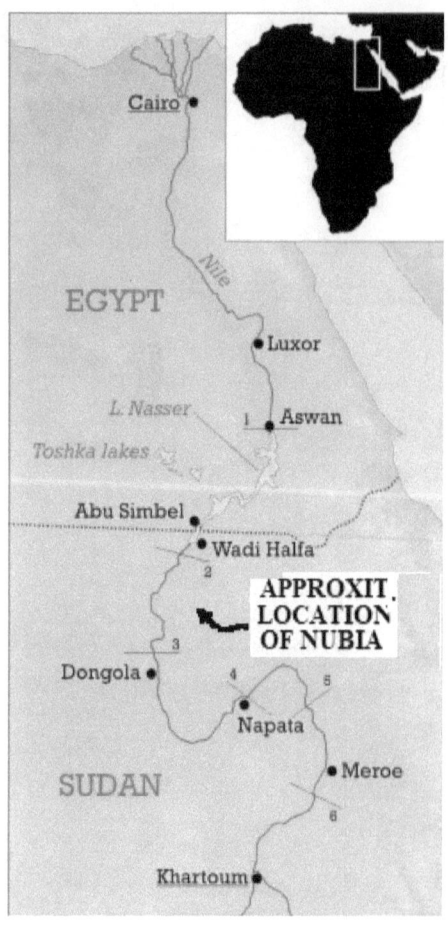

the wall, shows where this kingdom would have been. That is somewhere around Abu Simbel, a little bit north of it and south of it in the actual country of Sudan. Nubia was known to the Egyptians as Ta Sety, the Land of the Bow. Their warriors were ferocious and were feared by those who saw them in battles. Their weapon of choice was the bow. This type of weaponry was unknown to the Egyptians until then.

Although a simple soldier without any rank, Vas Nu Pieds immediately understood the importance of this new weaponry. He fought with courage, and the battle was barely won by the Egyptians that were armed only with spears. Vas Nu Pieds took a few bows and arrows from dead Nubian soldiers. And as soon as he got back from the battle, he promoted the fabrication of similar weaponry for the Egyptian Armed Forces.

Soon the king of the Hittites challenged the pharaoh again. The Hittite state, which was located northeast from Egypt, was at this time a small country that was very ambitious, and it wanted to build their country into an empire. That was the opportunity for the Egyptian army to use for the first time the new weaponry that Vas Nu Pieds inspired. The new weaponry constituted of bows and arrows as developed by Vas Nu Pieds. The Egyptian army won this war fast, leaving the Hittites in complete disarray. Never before had they fought an army using bows and arrows. As a result, the Hittites signed a treaty with Egypt, and the two countries exchanged letters and gifts and they became friends for some time. This raised the star of Vas Nu Pieds immediately, and the pharaoh invited him to come and see him.

Your dad greeted Vas Nu Pieds very warmly and he asked him much about himself and where he came from. Vas Nu Pieds was very frank about his background and told the pharaoh his whole story. The pharaoh invited the farmer who Vas Nu Pieds worked for to meet with him. The farmer was very scared of speaking with the pharaoh, but being an honest man, he revealed to the pharaoh that the story Vas Nu Pieds told was true and that since then, unfortunately, his wife, now his ex-wife, played the same game again with another young farm boy. But this time, he witnessed the two of them in the act.

He had gone to the village judge to ask for advice, and the judge, after consulting with the temple priest, suggested he give his wife a choice. The choice was that either she get divorced and be condemned to slavery or get divorced but spend the rest of her days as a servant in the temple of the goddess Maat, where there is an altar for the goddess Teny Te'en, the goddess of marital fidelity. And that is

MAAT EGYPTIAN GODDESS OF JUSTICE AND THE DIVINE ORDER

where she is now, serving for the rest of her life.

The pharaoh was pleased on by the honesty of the farmer and by the virtue of Vas Nu Pieds. So he decided to promote Vas Nu Pieds and make him a general. Humbled by the honor, Vas Nu Pieds vowed not to forget his humble origins and decided to go barefoot to all his battles from then on. He became known since then as the barefooted general.

"'And now, my beloved Khouf,' said my grandmother, 'since then, Vas Nu Pieds found himself fighting the Ribou tribe several times (this tribe lived where modern-time Libya is located). This tribe joined the Meshwesh tribe and tried once more to invade Egypt. Vas Nu Pieds defeated them for good this time. That is why he was invited today to come to the. audience hall to be honored by the pharaoh and by the whole country for this brave and victorious battle.'

"'Now I have to leave you, Khouf, as the time has come in the agenda for the grand vizier to invite General Vas Nu Pieds to enter the audience hall. Bye, my beloved Khouf, and never forget the love that your grandmother always has for you and will always continue to have.'

"'Goodbye, Grandma. Thank you for coming to help me,' I said.

"With these words, my grandmother just disappeared the same way as she appeared on my lap.

"Kendall, I was still getting out of my torpor, attempting to believe what just happened to me and that I was not dreaming, when the grand vizier loudly announced to the pharaoh and to the audience attending the meeting that a very important part of the agenda was about to take place. He introduced the subject by reminding the audience that General Vas Nu Pieds just returned, victorious from his war with the two tribes east of the country. He named these two tribes as the Ribou and the Meshwesh. He then explained that they formed an alliance and attempted to invade the north of the country. General Vas Nu Pieds, at the head of the Egyptian Armed Forces, defeated them and returned with the heads of these two tribes as prisoners and with a large number of these tribes' soldiers as prisoners of war. My father then asked the grand vizier if the general was in town.

"'Oh yes, Your Majesty,' answered the grand vizier. 'He's not only in town but has also asked me to request from Your Majesty the honor of being received by you to present his respect and bring to you the spoils of war of these battles with these two tribes.'

"'Invite him to the audience hall,' my father told the grand vizier.

"The grand vizier then asked one of the chamberlains to leave and invite General Vas Nu Pieds to enter the audience hall. There was a moment of silence and anticipation, then the main entrance door of the audience hall opened, and the chamberlain announced with pomp the entrance of General Vas Nu Pieds. The general entered the hall alone, walking slowly toward the pharaoh. And when he was close enough to the pharaoh, he kneeled and presented his respects, keeping his head bowed and without raising his eyes to the pharaoh.

"'Stand up, General Vas Nu Pieds,' said my dad, the pharaoh. You brought honor and pride to me, to the throne of Egypt, and to all your countrymen.'

"'I am your humble servant, Your Majesty,' replied Vas Nu Pieds. 'It was an honor for me to fight the enemies of Egypt and of Your Majesty's throne. Further, Your Divine Majesty, I feel proud of our soldiers, the sons of this great country of ours. I owe this victory to the courage and determination of our soldiers who did not hesitate to sacrifice their lives to defend their country. I am thrilled, Your Majesty, to bring to your feet as slaves the heads of the Ribou and the Meshwesh tribes, as well as a great number of their soldiers, to be dealt with as Your Majesty will decide to do. These tribes were defeated once and for all, and they will never dare to threaten our country again.'

"My father then asked General Vas Nu Pieds to come up the platform where we were sitting. The general obliged, and my father stood up and went to him in a gesture that was extraordinary, since the pharaoh was a deity. He took General Vas Nu Pieds in his arms and embraced him.

"All the people in the assembly hall were stunned and astonished in disbelief that their god, the pharaoh of Egypt, would honor someone the way my dad honored General Vas Nu Pieds. He then asked the general to sit in the empty chair next to him. As the general was hesitant in doing so, saying it was too much of an honor that he did not deserve, my dad insisted, and he obliged. Then my dad turned toward the grand vizier and told him to take note.

"'I want to grant General Vas Nu Pieds, out of my belongings, a large farm—as large as the one he was working in when he was working as a farmer in the rich man's farm. And I want all the prisoners he brought from the tribes of Ribou and Meshwesh to work there as the slaves of General Vas Nu Pieds.'

"He then turned toward the general and told him, 'All my family, my wife, brothers, and sisters are all admiring your courage and much more especially your virtuous conduct in life.'

"He also told him, 'I have a message from my bachelor sister. Because I also concur with my sister's request, I have accepted to transmit to you, General Vas Nu Pieds, my sister's message. The message is that my sister admires you very much and is falling in love with you. Knowing that you are a virtuous man, she is offering to be your wife if you, General Vas Nu Pieds, are not involved with someone else.'

"'Oh, my master and god,' said Vas Nu Pieds.

"There the pharaoh interrupted him, saying, 'I know that it is too much for you to absorb in such a short time. Please just think about it, and I would like you to come and have a meal with me and my family tomorrow at noon. And we shall discuss this and other matters and plans I have for you.'

"With that and without giving a chance for Vas Nu Pieds to respond, he turned to the people assembled there and started to applaud. Immediately, all the people in the assembly hall applauded and kept applauding as the pharaoh took my hand and left the assembly hall.

"The pharaoh leaving this way was really an extraordinary event. Immediately, chamberlains, seat holder's men, soldiers assigned to guard the pharaoh, and other noble people who normally escort the pharaoh ran to their positions to do what was expected of them when the pharaoh moves. The same thing happened with the people assigned to escort me, the pharaoh's son, to and from the great hall. It was quite confusing. After a moment, at the orders of the pharaoh's chamberlain, the pharaoh's escort procession was followed by my escort's procession. Once more, my dad confused the protocol by deciding to walk back to our private part of the palace, having me next to him and holding my hand. Again more confusion as my dad started to laugh loudly. He directed his escort's procession to go ahead of us and my escort procession to follow us. That way, we walked together as my dad started to talk to me about his plans for the lunch invitation for Vas Nu Pieds. He was really excited to have these moments with him in a family setting. He knew well of his humble origin and of his extraordinary climb up the political scale, and he told me that the people of Egypt would be so proud to see one of them going all the way up there because of his virtue and military courage.

"That was a moment of great pride for me. I felt my dad—the pharaoh, my dad, the god of Egypt, my dada, man and god, so generous and so human—was the greatest in the world. I still think so today, even after so many centuries after his death. Oh yes, he was, and I loved him so much. You should know how that feels as I know you also, Kendall, love and admire your dad very, very much."

6 The Wedding Banquet of My Aunt and of the General

"As we were walking, Dad started to tell me what he was planning to do for the luncheon for Vas Nu Pieds.

"'I want to invite all his relatives and friends, the great priests, the grand vizier, other important people, and all the other army generals. I want to have a bull slaughtered and the bull meat served as part of the meal.'

"That was, in ancient Egypt, one of the great honors that could be given in a celebration, as meat was rarely served except in very important occasions.

"'I want the grand priest of the Karnack temple to be there too. That is, in case that Vas Nu Pieds and my sister decide to marry right away. I have plans to have dancers for this lunch. I will ask my wife and my sister to choose who they want as maids of honor, as well as what they want for the wedding dresses of my wife and of my bride-to-be sister.'

"As he was voicing all his day's dreaming to me, we finally arrived in our quarters of the palace. There, my mom, his sister, and other women related to us were waiting for us. As soon as they saw us, they began to sing and dance and ululate with joy

COOKS IN THE PHARAOH KITCHEN

and pleasure."

"Wait a minute," said Kendall, interrupting my enthusiastic talk to her. "What does ululate mean?"

"Ah," responded Khouf, "you don't have that in your culture. Back then, in ancient Egypt as well as now in Egypt and many other countries around Egypt, women demonstrate their joy and pleasure by emitting loud, sustained, and trilling sounds of joy. It is from these kinds of sounds that the English word alleluia came and is used in Christian and Judaic liturgies to express great joy.

"Now back to what I was telling you. I did not know at first that most of this hullabaloo was in my honor because I was returning from my first official event with my dad.

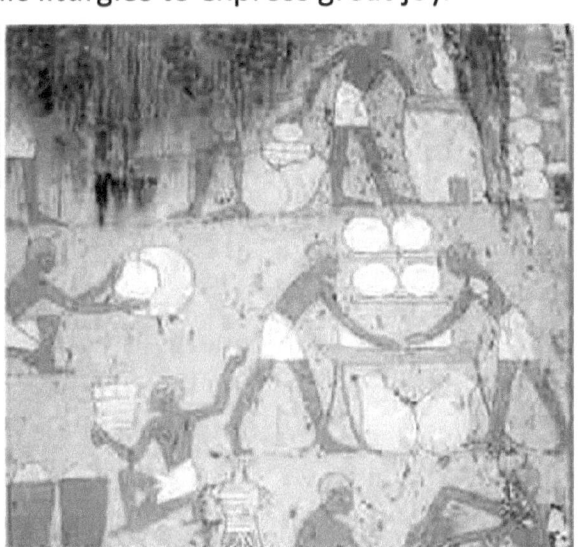

BAKERS IN THE PHARAOH KITCHEN

"My dad then told my mom and the family, 'I invited Vas Nu Pieds for lunch to meet my sister, and I have plans for the general and my sister to marry.'

"'What!' said his sister.

"'Yes,' my dad answered, laughing his head off. 'You told me of your admiration and your feelings for this man, and I told him what you felt. He was elated and even blushed. So I decided that according to our traditions, you should marry each other, maybe as soon as during this lunch.'

"'What?' said his sister again, blushing. 'My brother, you could have at least consulted with me. What if I am not ready to marry yet?'

"'Oh,' said my dad, 'really? So do you want me to cancel the lunch and apologize to the general for what I said? And that will be the end of it.'

WOMAN PLAYIG THE HARP DURING A WEDDING

"'No, no,' said my aunt. 'I will abide with the wish of my brother and king. As you are also god on earth, your wish is my order.'

"'Ha ha ha.' The pharaoh laughed. 'I am glad you agree with me. And I know you will be a great wife to Vas Nu Pieds and that you will also be a happy and fulfilled woman with this union. Now let's get to work to make this lunch and wedding a wonderful event.'

"Then he instructed one of the servants to call on Chamberlain Kar Tu Mow to come and see him right away. Then he turned to my mom and asked her, 'Darling wife, please group all the house servants and instruct them to prepare a banquet—one that would have to please the gods.

Please also invite all our family living with us in the pharaoh's quarters, including all my wives and all the other ladies living with them. Also make sure that the court seamstresses get busy immediately and start preparing an adequate nuptial dress for my sister. I also want you to be my sister's maid of honor and decide with my sister on who else she would like to have as bridesmaids. She also has to decide how she wants the wedding dresses to be.'

"You know, Kendall, that in our customs, the bride and the bridesmaids wear similar dresses in order to confuse evil spirits. My dad also asked my mom to have wedding bouquets prepared. The wedding bouquets also in our customs had to be made of thyme and garlic to keep evil spirits away. Finally, he assigned my mom to select the dancers and the music for the wedding.

"My mother then left and went to group the house servants and to take care of all these tasks. My dad and I were there alone for a few minutes. Then Chamberlain Kar Tu Mow arrived precipitously. He bowed to my dad and me, saying, 'At your orders, milord.'

"My dad greeted him then asked, 'Chamberlain Kar Tu Mow, I want you to go and invite the grand priest of the Karnack temple and his family to come and have lunch tomorrow with me and my family. Let him also know that the invitation is for the wedding of my sister. Also request the grand priest of the Karnack temple to come and see me in the throne room as soon as possible.'

"The throne room, Kendall is part of the rooms directly at the service of the pharaoh.

As you may remember, this room is that very small private chapel dedicated to the god Amun-Ra. That is where my dad, the pharaoh, asked the grand priest to join him in prayers to meet with the gods. It is room No. 5 in the palace plan that was described earlier to you.

"Kendall, my dad also told the chamberlain to invite in his name the chief of staff of the armed forces to come and have lunch tomorrow with him and his family and to let him know that the invitation was for the wedding of his sister. He also told the chamberlain to request that the chief of staff of the armed forces to comes and see him as soon as possible.

"He then took my hand in his, and the two of us went to the throne room. I was very impressed, as this was the first time I was allowed in this room. There my dad introduced me to the gods, and the two of us remained sitting in silence, waiting for something to happen. What first broke our silence was the arrival of the grand priest of the Karnak temple. He entered in silence with a small boy dressed in a gold dress. The grand priest sat next to my dad, and the boy went next to the statue of the god Amun-Ra. Now the three of us were there waiting. Honestly, first I did not know what we were waiting for, and I started to feel impatient in this dark room facing the statues of the god Amun-Ra and that kid next to the statue. Then all of a sudden, we heard noises like thunder and saw like lightning in the room, and we heard a grave voice saying, 'I am Amun-Ra. What brings you here, Pharaoh, with the grand priest? And is this young man your son that you introduced to me when he was born?'

"The grave voice was coming from the mouth of the young kid.

"My father then answered, 'Oh, you, Amun-Ra, king of all gods, we are here to ask you for your blessings for us, for my sister, your humble servant, who will get married tomorrow, and for General Vas Nu Pieds, who will be her husband.'

"Then we heard through the voice of the little boy, 'Oh, Pharaoh, living incarnation of Horus on earth, I give you and yours my blessing and will request in your name as well as in mine that Isis, goddess of motherhood and

MUSICIANS IN PHARAOHS COURT

marital devotion, bestow also her blessing in your sister and her husband-to-be. I will also ask Bes, the god of love and marriage, to bless this wedding. I will ask the gods and goddesses of fertility—Apis, Hator, Ken, Mut, Osiris, Qetesh, Satis, Selket, and Taueret—to bestow on your sister and Vas Nu Pieds to provide your family with many healthy children. My blessing and all gods' blessings are on you and on your loved ones.'

"Then the room illuminated as if the sun was right there, to the point that one could not look at the statue of Amun-Ra without being blinded by the light. And then the room was back as it was when we entered it. That was the time that my dad, the grand priest, the young kid, and I left the room. Once outside the room, my dad reiterated the invitation to his sister's wedding and asked the grand priest to perform the wedding.

"The grand priest bowed to my dad and told him he was honored to officiate at the wedding of the sister of Hatus on earth and would do so. As we were walking toward our home, I asked my dad why so many gods and the god of fertility were named by the god Amun-Ra. 'Well,' my dad answered me, 'in our culture, it is very important that once married, the couple must produce many children. Each of these gods or goddesses are known for helping this happen.'

"The next morning, the palace was like a beehive. The cooks in the kitchen were busy producing all kinds of delicacies. All kinds of dishes were prepared—dishes of butter and cheese and dishes of fattened fowl and beef. They smelled so good and were so appetizing as they were flavored with rosemary, cumin, garlic, parsley, cinnamon, and mustard, and were sweetened with honey, figs, and other fruits. In addition to the beef dishes, the cooks prepared dishes with duck, geese, goats, fish, and pigs. Plates were filled with chickpeas and lentils, lettuce, cucumbers, and onions. They prepared about fifteen varieties of bread that could be served. There was also wine and beer, and

A DOUBLE PIPER PLAYER AND WOMEN CLAPPERS IN A WEDDING

plenty of it. There were jugs with the date and type of wine, the estate where it was stored, the vineyard, and the vintner.

No expenses were spared for my aunt's wedding meal. "Leaving the kitchen, I was astonished to see what was happening to the large court where I used to play with my friends. There were little tables and benches all over the court. Over each table were already bowls, plates, and cups made from blue faience with lotus designs over them. Jugs of wine and beer were on each table. Well-dressed servant girls in very pretty dresses carried trays laden with delicacies and were ready for the guests' arrivals.

In one corner of the court next to where a platform was erected to be as a stage was a woman playing the harp all by herself. She was also fixing the harp's cords in preparation for the background music she would be playing during the wedding ceremony. During the lunch preceding the wedding ceremony, she would join the remaining musicians for the concert they would be giving. The palace musicians were using many instruments. Many of these instruments were similar to the ones your people use these days. However, the most basic instruments were per-

HARP PLAYER AND DANCERS IN A WEDDING IN PHARAOH PALACE

cussion, and the simplest of these were human hands used for clapping. Other forms of percussion instruments, such as drums in the shape of a goblet and wheel-thrown pots with skin-covered tops and open bottoms, were also used. There was also the sistrum, which was a metal rattle or noisemaker, consisting of a handle and a frame fitted with loosely held rods that could be jingled. The band also used symbols consisting of a pair of concave discs of about six inches across that were attached to the player's hand with leather straps. These musicians also used wind and string instruments. The wind instruments included flutes, parallel double pipes, and divergent double pipes. They also used trumpets that were made of silver and bronze, with mouthpieces of gold or silver, and lyre and harps, as well as lutes similar to today's mandolins.

"Around twelve noon, everything appeared to be ready for the guests and for General Vas Nu Pieds's arrival. And indeed, a few moments later, they started to arrive. Both my mom and dad warmly welcomed each guest. Most of the guests were flabbergasted for being received by the pharaoh himself. They have never experienced such reception or such an honor before. Upon entering the party, a group of very attractive young women draped

WOMEN DANCERS DANCING AND PLAYING INSTRUMENTS DURING A WEDDING

each of the guests in blossoms and fragrant wreaths of flowers. They also placed perfumed wax cones on the guest's heads. The heat of their bodies slowly melted the scented wax through the evening until the perfumed wax would filter through the hair or the wig of the guest. The scent of the wreaths of flowers mingled with the perfumed wax cones.

These same young women directed the guests to their assigned tables. There they sat on benches. Soon scantily clad servant girls served them delicacies. These girls carried trays filled with rich dishes of butter and cheese, as well as figs and other fruits. The guests picked up these hors d'oeuvres and placed them in plates made from blue faience. Other girls carried jugs of beer and wine and served the guests either beer or wine as they wished.

"I was not asked to join my parents in welcoming the guests. I was asked to sit in a table not too far from where the pharaoh and the guests of honor would sit. Around me in my table were all the young children of the court and my cousins and half-brothers and sisters. From where I was, I could see all that was going on at the entrance of the court and in most places of the court. Next to me was my wonderful and sweet friend, Mangie. Remember her? Her real name was Mange Ta Soupe. We were talking and laughing and also a little bit flirting. As for me, she was a very special person, and I liked her very much. I held her hand, and as I was talking either to her or to other kids at our table, I was gently caressing her hand. When I was glancing at her, she was blushing, but obviously she was enjoying having her hand in mine. And she was also caressing my fingers gently and sweetly. Oh, I felt like I was in heaven next to her.

"Soon a great commotion took place at the entrance of the palace court. Everyone's attention was directed to where the pharaoh and his wife were, as they were welcoming the guests. That was when General Vas Nu Pieds arrived. He was dressed in the official dress of a general of the pharaoh's army. He was tall and very handsome in his uniform. Accompanying the general was a very old

HARP PLAYER AND DANCERS IN A
WEDDING IN PHARAOH PALACE

man with long hair, a long beard, and thick eyebrows. This was Old Man River, whom the general introduced to the pharaoh and his wife, apologizing for taking the liberty of bringing this man with him. He then told the pharaoh that he owed this old man all that he had achieved in life. He told the pharaoh that he was indebted to him and did not know how he could ever show enough gratitude for what he did for him. He also emphasized that without the help and advice of this man, he would not have entered the service of the pharaoh. The pharaoh very graciously welcomed the general's guest and greeted the general as well as his guest. Then the pharaoh himself directed Vas Nu Pieds and his guest to the table of honor, where they were to sit in the company of the pharaoh, his wife, and his sister. On their way to the table, Vas Nu Pieds kept talking to the pharaoh.

"'Your Divine Majesty,' said he, 'the reason I brought Old Man River with me is to beg you to help him undo a curse initiated fifteen years ago by the grand priest of the Karnak temple. Here is his story.'

"'Old Man River was a priest in the temple of Aton during the reign of Pharaoh Akhenaton. When this pharaoh passed away, as you know, the person who was the grand priest of the Karnack temple at that time became the young pharaoh's tutor. For all practical purposes, he took over the country and controlled the young pharaoh, who was a very young man with no experience. As he ruled the country, he banned Aton's cult and anything dealing with this religion. As Old Man River insisted on keeping his faith, contrary to the wish of the new religious power, he was given a choice to either to renounce his faith of else.

"'Well, he did not renounce his faith. The grand priest banned him from all temples and condemned him to wander alone in woods around the Nile River.

To survive, Old Man River had to hunt and fish for food. As he protested this harsh treatment, the grand priest of the Karnack temple called on a famous sorcerer who was living there and asked him to curse him. The curse made sure that Old Man River would remain living in this forest among rags and animals and birds for the rest of his life and that should he ever shave his head, beard, or his eyebrows, he would suffer a sickness that will cause great pain all over his body, handicapping him forever.'

"'For heaven's sake,' reacted the pharaoh. 'This is a terrible revenge and was not warranted. Fortunately, the actual grand priest of the Karnack temple is a more hu-

'PROFESSIONAL DANCERS DANCING IN WEDDINGS & SPECIALS EVENTS

mane and reasonable man. Let me see how we can undo this and free your friend and benefactor from this terrible curse.'

"'Oh, thank you so much, Your Divine Majesty. I will be indebted to you for my entire life, as this man helped me and led me to become who I am now as your servant and the general of your armed forces.'

"By then, they arrived at the pharaoh's table. There, Vas Nu Pieds bowed very respectfully and saluted the pharaoh's sister and greeted her pompously, calling her sister. In ancient Egypt, the most affectionate titles you could call a person you love was brother or sister. Naturally, this had nothing to do with sibling relations. This was despite the fact that in the nobility of this time, it often occurred that brothers and sisters got married to each other. When that occurred, it was often for reasons of state or to keep power and or wealth in the confines of the family.

"Nanouka, the pharaoh's sister, returned the general's greetings, also referring to him as her brother. That im-

mediately established a loving and friendly rapport between the two of them. She added to her salutation that
she always admired his courage and the way she was told
he comported himself in war and as a victorious general.
The general then complimented her for her looks, telling
her that she was as pretty and as romantic as the moon
was in a summer night.

Looking her in the eyes, he added that her beauty glit-
tered as millions of Amun-Ra exposed to the sun's rays in
a spring day. She smiled, blushed, and was very pleased
by the way things were turning out. She was indeed very
attractive as she wore a long dress or tunic made of linen,
which was covered from head to toe with bead nets. The
entire dress was enhanced with gold, silver, and lapis
necklaces. She wore a necklace and bracelets of emerald
and other Amun-Ra jewelry over her chest.

"What follows may seem strange to you, Kendall, but it
should not be. The family of the couple getting married,
especially in the upper classes, arranged most marriages.
Many couples did fall in love first and choose each other
as mates, and then the family of the couple took the next
steps. Although most of the time, women played a large
role in arranging a marriage. This time, it was the pharaoh
himself who did so. Egyptians held marriages as a sacred
bond. For us, Kendall, a marriage was a lifelong monoga-
mous relationship. Entering into a marriage was described as 'making a wife' or 'taking a wife,' but it seems
that the girl's father, and in this case, the girl's brother
who was the pharaoh, had the main say, since the girl had
no father and the pharaoh was her brother and also the
ruler of the country.

"The pharaoh, or more exactly my mom in this case,

made sure that Vas Nu Pieds and my aunt were sitting next to each other. They were conversing with sweet words, sometimes flirting, sometimes joking. All through the conversations around the table, servant girls with trays filled with delicacies were serving all the guests, who were eating those delightful hors d'oeuvres. My father looked around to make sure everyone from his household was at the wedding. He could not find his Syrian wife, Merdonice. She was hard not to be seen as she was quite young and very attractive. He discreetly called his chamberlain, Kar Tu Mow, and asked him to go and find out where Merdonice was and if she was safe and well. Then, with a gesture of his hand, the pharaoh instructed the band of musicians to start the music. Until that time, the only music heard consisted of a harp player playing background music. Immediately, the music heard became a full orchestra concert. Dancers also started to dance on the floor between the tables, enchanting the participants with their gracious undulations.

"Soon Vas Nu Pieds and Nanouka were using their first names as they talked to each other, and they had their arms around each other's waists. As the lunch was advancing, they started to hold hands and offered each other flowers and food. Love and affection were very rapidly developing between these two lovebirds.

"That was the time that my dad chose to intervene.

"'What do you think, you lovebirds?' he said. 'Would you like to be married?'

"'Oops!' Vas Nu Pieds and my aunt all of a sudden became self-conscious and blushed. They looked at each other and smiled. They were holding hands, and one could see that these two hands squeezed each other a little harder. But they really did not know what to say. It was obvious to all that the answer would be yes—that is, if they were not taken by surprise with my dad's question.

"Realizing the odd situation, my dad added, 'In our customs, it is the parents who arrange marriages. Since I am the parent, and it is abundantly clear to me that the two of you are ready to be each other's mates, I will call on the grand priest of the temple of Karnack who is with us at this table to go ahead and perform the wedding ceremony.'

"With a gesture from my dad, the band stopped playing, and the dancers discreetly stopped dancing then left the stage. And only the harpist continued playing. Hers was a very soft music, almost like background music.

"The grand priest of the temple of Karnack stood up, left the table, and went on the stage. Then he invited Vas Nu Pieds and my aunt to join him. He asked them to sit on two seats that looked like thrones, pretty much like the picture that is opposite this text, and had the three of them facing the audience, who suddenly became silent, anticipating the event. He also asked the bridesmaids to join them on the stage.

SITTING ARRANGEMENT FOR BRIDE & GROOM
DURING WEDDING CEREMONY

"Bridesmaids and brides wore similar dresses in order to confuse evil spirits. The original wedding bouquets were made of thyme and garlic to keep evil spirits away.

"Then the grand priest of the temple of Karnack started talking in a loud voice and said, 'As the Hemu of the Isis goddess, I am authorized to perform the religious ceremony and ritual that will make you husband and wife. Therefore, I will proceed in joining you in holy matrimony. And in accordance to our ancient traditions and religion, the two of you as of now are expected to love and respect each other.'

"Then he took a small piece of hemp, gave each end to Vas Nu Pieds and my aunt, and asked them to wave the hemp around them. He then produced a wedding ring also made by weaving hemp into a circle and then asked Vas Nu Pieds to repeat after him.

"'I, Vas Nu Pieds, general of the Pharaoh Amenhotep, take thee, Nanouka, to be my wife and my queen, to share the good times and hard times side by side. I humbly give you my hand and my heart as I pledge my faith and love to you. Just as this ring I give you today is a circle without end, my love for you is eternal. Just as it is made of incorruptible substance, my commitment to you will never fail. With this ring, I thee wed you.'

"Once Vas Nu Pieds finished his vows, the grand priest of the temple of Karnack asked my aunt to repeat after him: 'I, Nanouka, sister of the great pharaoh Amenhotep, take thee, Vas Nu Pieds, to be my husband and my king, to share the good times and hard times side by side. I humbly give you my hand and my heart as I pledge my faith and love to you.

Just as this ring I give you today is a circle without end,

my love for you is eternal. Just as it is made of incorruptible substance, my commitment to you will never fail. With this ring, I thee wed you.'

ONE OF THE DANCERS DANCING AT THE WEDDING OF VAS NU PIEDS & NANOUKA SISTER OF THE PHARAOH

"The two of them were asked to sign the contract of their marriage, and the pharaoh and his wife signed it too as the witnesses. "

At this time, Chamberlain Kar Tu Mow returned and whispered in the pharaoh's ear. I learned later on that he told him that his wife Merdonice isolated herself with the priest whose name was Twistmind in a private room. The room's door was guarded, and the meeting there was supposed to be secret.

"The pharaoh thanked Chamberlain Kar Tu Mow, then he moved toward the newlyweds and did something very unusual.

He turned around and asked Old Man River to come up and join them on the stage, and he asked him to also sign the contract of marriage. Turning to the audience, he then explained that if this poor old-looking man had not made a very generous and risky gesture to help Vas Nu Pieds when he was in distress, what they were witnessing would have never happened. The audience applauded, and poor Old Man River was embarrassed and was trying

WOMEN PLAYING MUSIC INSTRUMENTS IN WEDDINGS

to kiss the hand of Vas Nu Pieds and the feet of the pharaoh.

"The marriage contract contained the date (the year of the reign of the pharaoh Amenhotep), the name of Vas Nu Pieds, the names of the pharaoh (as the brother of Nanouka) and of Old Man River (as the foster father of Vas Nu Pieds), Vas Nu Pieds's profession, the name of the grand priest of the temple of Karnak, the name of the scribe who drew up the contract, and the names of Pharaoh Amenhotep and Old Man River as witnesses.

"The finished document was given to the grand priest of the temple of Karnack for safekeeping and kept the records at Amun-Ra's safe room of the Karnack temple. When the wedding formalities were completed, the pharaoh called for continuing the celebration in honor of the united couple. He turned around and faced the musicians and shouted, 'Let the music begin!'

"Immediately, male and female dancers and musicians

started the music and their dances. They brought excitement to the festivity with harps, lyres, and lutes. Female musicians played a type of oboe to keep up the beat of the music and the hearts of the guests. Dancing girls wearing jewels treated the guests. Acrobats who twisted, jumped, and turned were all over the place. The musicians also encouraged the guests to join in by chanting, clapping, or playing tambourines or cymbals.

"It was quite a show and quite a party, Kendall. I still remember it as if it were yesterday, and I still remember how much I enjoyed it.

"After the contract of the wedding was signed, Nanouka and her new husband, Vas Nu Pieds, sat next to each other in a sofa-like armchair, very close to each other and leaning affectionately, caressing each other tenderly. My aunt had that silly smile on her face that meant that she was almost in heaven in the arms of her husband, and Vas Nu Pieds with his arms around her could not believe he was awake and not dreaming, and his happiness and satisfaction was just so overwhelming that he thought he was in another world. He was happy and so full of love and attention for his new bride.

"The two of them, still holding hands, asked the goddess Isis to bless their union and marriage and to give them many children. They did this in accordance with the customs of the upper class of the Egyptian rulers.

"As the evening advanced and was now late in the night, the guests started to leave. Vas Nu Pieds told Nanouka that he brought with him a few girls that would be her servants and helpers from then on for anything she may want to have or want to have done for her. They came prepared to move her belongings to her new home with her husband.

"My aunt Nanouka was also ready for the move. She asked her servants, all six of them, to assemble the trunks containing her

DANCERS IN WEDDINGS DURING THE PHARAHONIC TIME

belongings and personal effects. The six women disappeared into the private quarters of my aunt and found there the girls that Vas Nu Pieds brought with him to assist my aunt in her moving. When all the trunks and other effects were ready, a few male servants moved these trunks and other stuff belonging to my aunt to several wheeled vehicles that were waiting there to move my aunt's stuff to her new home. Once these tasks were completed, it was time for the newlyweds to leave for their home. Vas Nu Pieds and his wife went to my dad, the pharaoh, to thank him and leave for their new home.

"My dad apologized to Nanouka, telling her, 'Before the two of you leave me, I have to undertake with your husband one more important task.'

"Then my dad took Vas Nu Pieds with him and asked one servant to go and get Old Man River, as well as the grand priest of the Karnack temple. When the three of us arrived, my dad led all of us toward the throne room, which was, as I told you before, a private temple to the god Amun-Ra. My dad, the grand priest, and the small boy that came with the grand priest entered the temple as we were waiting outside.

GODDESS ISIS
GODDESS OF MARIAGE, FERTILITY AND MOTHERHOOD

"A few minutes later, the grand priest came out of the temple and invited Old Man River and me to join him inside the temple. As far as I know, that was a first, as the only people that were allowed in this temple were the pharaoh, and occasionally, with special permission of the god, his son, as the heir of the throne, and the grand priest of the temple of Karnack. As we were getting inside the temple, the grand priest reminded us, and me in particular, not to talk until asked to do so by either my dad or the god. He also told me that I had to remain very attentive to the talks and to whatever instructions that we could be given. Once in this small temple, we were directed to stand along a sidewall, as my dad and the priest were facing the statue of the god Amun-Ra. The boy went next to the statue of the god Amun-Ra.

"The temple was dark, and there was a deafening silence. Suddenly, the room was illuminated like the sun itself was in the room. We almost had to cover our eyes with our hands so as not to be dazzled by the brightness of such light. Then we heard the voice of the god Amun-Ra through the mouth of the boy, saying, 'Amenhotep, Amenhotep, now that I allowed your son and this man, this friend of yours, in my presence, tell me what brought you all here.'

"'I am here, oh god of all gods, to beg your help on a matter of great importance to our country and also to redress an injustice committed many years ago by a revengeful sorcerer. This man I brought to you is actually known as Old Man River. He was a priest in the temple of Aton when the pharaoh Akhenaton was alive. When this pharaoh passed away and rejoined the family of gods many years ago, the grand priest of the Karnack temple took over the country and controlled the pharaoh, who was then a very young man with no experience, and he banned the Aton cult and anything dealing with this religion. As he insisted on keeping his faith, contrary to the wish of the new religious power, he was given a choice to either renounce his faith or else.'

"'He did not renounce his faith. He was then banned from all temples and was condemned to wander alone in the adjacent woods, hunting and fishing for food. As he protested this harsh treatment, the grand priest of the Karnack temple called on Sohounac, who was a famous sorcerer that was living there and asked him to do his thing. His thing was a curse. And the curse made sure that he would, for the rest of his life, live in this forest among rags, animals, and birds. Further, he was told that if he ever shaved his head, his beard, and his eyebrows like any priest must do, he would suffer of a sickness that will cause great pain all over his body, and he will be handicapped forever. He was well received by the forest's animals, and soon he was communicating with them in their languages. Therefore, he never hunted for food and went fishing to feed himself.'

"'That was when Vas Nu Pieds, then a poor laborer in a rich man's farm, met Old Man River. He was running from his master's wife's lust and revenge for refusing to comply with her desire. Vas Nu Pieds and Old Man River exchanged their stories. Old Man River helped his new friend by providing food and lodging in the forest and advised him to join the pharaoh's army, which he did. The rest is history. Vas Nu Pieds became a most victorious general, and he is now my brother-in-law. He owes a debt of love and of gratitude to this man, and he wants him to be part of his family as a foster father.'

"The voice of the god Amun-Ra came from the small boy's mouth, and again he said, 'Amenhotep, living incarnation of Horus, I want to grant you your wish, and I will. However, you must be very careful as Sohounac is still alive and is a very mean creature. He has no power over my word, but he is a very revengeful person. If and when he knows what I am about to do for you, he will be after your family and your descendants. He may not directly reach you, but he befriended several wicked gods that could cause harm to your loved ones.'

"Then the voice of the god Amun-Ra, coming from the little boy's mouth, addressed me said, 'Khouf, be careful in your life. You may not know it, but you are surrounded by evil creatures that want to harm you. Neither you nor Pharaoh Amenhotep, your dad, is aware of who they are. Be aware. There is a nest of vipers in the palace. Do you hear me, Amenhotep and Khouf? Sohounac may find his way to them and could use the power of his friends, the wicked gods, to achieve his evil goals.'

"After a short silence, the god Amun-Ra addressed Old Man River. He said, 'As of now, Old Man River, I grant you pardon for whatever offense you may have done to the grand priest of the temple of Karnack and provide you with protection from any evil resulting from Sohounac, the sorcerer. Go shave your head, shave your beard, and feel free to go and live your life in the household of General Vas Nu Pieds. You shall be blessed for your action for him, and as his foster father, you should enjoy life with his family.'

"At this time, the throne room darkened, and my dad gestured to Old Man River that it was time to leave, and he took my hand and we left the throne room.

"Vas Nu Pieds was waiting outside the room. He saw us leaving the throne room. Old Man River, with a great smile and with his two arms open, invited Vas Nu Pieds for a hug. Indeed, they hugged, and Old Man River told Vas Nu Pieds that he was free to shave his beard, his hair, and become again the reverend and faithful priest he was before the curse. The two of them held hands, and after thanking my dad and kneeling in respect to him, they ran out like children, still holding hands. They joined the caravan of Nanouka, who was waiting for her husband. Thus the newlyweds and their suite started to move to the home of Vas Nu Pieds.

"My dad, still holding my hand in his, had a very serious look on his face. When I asked why he was looking that way, he answered me, 'You heard the god Amun-Ra's words. These words still resonate in my head, as he does not give such warning very easily. "Be aware, Amenhotep and Khouf. There is a nest of vipers in the palace. Sohounac may find his way to them and could use the power of his friends to achieve his evil goals."'

"He also remembered that when he asked Chamberlain Kar Tu Mow to go and check where his Syrian wife was, he found out that she was secretly meeting with Twistmind. What was going on? He did not feel comfortable tying up these two pieces of information.

"We arrived at the scene of the wedding banquet, and now the room was almost empty. My mom was worried about where my dad and I were, but she was so relieved

GODDESS ISIS, GODDESS OF LOVE AND FERTILITY

to see us back, holding hands. She joined us, holding my dad's other hand, and we went to our private quarters.

"That was quite a day. We said good night to each other, and to bed we went."

7 The Calm Before the Storm

"And we kept walking silently, holding hands, my dad and I, first. And for some time I did not give too much importance to what my dad was worrying about. My dad, still with a very serious look on his face, said, 'I am worried about what the god Amun-Ra said. You heard these words, didn't you, Khouf?

"'These words still resonate in my head: "Be aware, Amenhotep and Khouf. There is a nest of vipers in the palace. Sohounac may find his way to them and could use the power of his friends to achieve his evil goals." Khouf, my son, the god Amun-Ra does not give such warnings easily.'

"My face may have looked like I did not know what my dad was talking about. My dad noticed it, and he explained, 'Son, Sohounac is the famous sorcerer called by the grand priest of the Karnak temple who cursed Old Man River and asked him to do his thing. His thing was a curse. And the curse made sure that he would remain for the rest of his life living in this forest among the animals and birds. Old Man River was to live like an animal for the rest of his life, living in this forest among the animals and birds. Further, he was told that if he ever shaved his head, his beard, and his eyebrows like any priest must do, he would suffer from a sickness that will cause great pain all over his body and will handicap him forever.'

"My father also told me, almost like a confidant, that when he asked Chamberlain Kar Tu Mow to go and check where his Syrian wife was, he found out that she was secretly meeting with Twistmind.

"He kept whispering to himself, 'What is going on? I do not feel comfortable tying up these two pieces of information.'

"When we arrived at the scene of the wedding banquet, we found the room almost empty. My mom was still there. She was sitting on a bench in the middle of room as the servants were cleaning the area after the celebration ended. She was so relieved to see us back, as she was worried about where my dad and I were. Dad took her hand, and the three of us went home. Dad kissed my mom and me, and then we went to his private area, where only he could sleep.

"I could not get over my dad's apprehension. I went to bed. And after the normal ritual I had to go through every night, I found myself thinking about what Dad told me in confidence.

"My dad was not feeling comfortable about something—that was news for me, very disturbing news, as I always perceived him to be above all worrying and having a solution for any problem. I finally went to sleep. The next morning, I woke up much earlier than usual, and looking outside, I saw Dad sitting by himself, looking very absorbed in his thinking. Instinctively, I joined him, and that was before the normal rituals that I had to go through every morning. I ran to my dad, and he opened his arms to hug me. We remained in each other's arms for a good and long moment, during which I felt so secure and at peace. Then my dad instructed me to go back and take care of my morning rituals and, once these were done, to come back to him. As I was leaving, I saw him instructing one of the servants, who was always around him to come closer to him, and he whispered some instructions that I did not hear.

"When I came back, I saw my father sitting there with

the grand priest of the Karnak temple and with Chamberlain Kar Tu Mow. The three of them were discussing a matter that sounded very serious to me. As I approached them, my dad realized I was there, and he invited me to join them. He told the two other interlocutors that since this matter might touch me in the future, he wanted me to listen to the discussion. That is why I can tell you the subject of their discussion today. Naturally, as you may have guessed, it was about what the god Amun-Ra told him and the finding that his Syrian wife, Merdonice, did not attend my aunt's wedding ceremony and secretly isolated herself with the priest whose name was Twistmind in a private room, with the room's door guarded. These two subjects, that apparently were not necessarily related, were tied up together in my dad's mind.

"Without going into the details of this discussion, the three men agreed with the pharaoh's decision to appoint a person who would secretly investigate what was going on between Twistmind and Merdonice. That was probably when the word *detective* was used for the first time. The detective's task was to find out as discreetly as possible what was really going on between Merdonice and Twistmind, other than what was readily or publicly accessible.

"My dad also wanted this detective to investigate all available information in the kingdom to establish that Sohounac, the famous sorcerer, was possibly related to Twistmind. He gave Chamberlain Kar Tu Mow the task of selecting the person that would be appointed to do these two tasks. He also asked Chamberlain Kar Tu Mow to call for a meeting in a few more days with the generals heading the three army's brigades in charge of protecting the frontiers of the country. And that was the end of that meeting. Then my dad turned to me and told me, 'Son, I want you to join me in this meeting and to listen to the information these generals will be providing.'

"For your knowledge, Kendall, a brigade is a large body of troops. This body is a tactical and administrative unit composed of a headquarters.

"A few days later, Chamberlain Kar Tu Mow asked to meet with the pharaoh. He wanted to give him the name of the person that he would recommend be appointed detective. This detective would investigate the situation that the pharaoh wanted to have investigated. That person was at one time an ambassador of Egypt to the king of Kadesh, and he was, at the same time, an undercover spy for the pharaoh. His name was Maha too. The pharaoh accepted and approved the chamberlain's selection. To avoid a delicate situation, it was the chamberlain who assigned the task to the detective.

"In the same meeting, Chamberlain Kar Tu Mow advised the pharaoh that he would have the generals heading the three army brigades back from their respective posts and available to report to the pharaoh at any time of his choice. He also asked, on behalf of the generals, if it was OK for these generals to bring assistants with them who could better describe the situation at the borders, provide details, and explain the different spies' reports. The pharaoh approved the chamberlain's request, and a meeting was set to take place at the large audience hall at the palace three days later to give all the generals and their assistants time to prepare.

"You remember, Kendall, the description I gave you of the palace where my dad and I lived? The large audience hall where this meeting would take place is shown in yellow in the partial plan of the palace.

"And the third day came before we knew it. Early in the morning, the large audience hall began to be filled with lots of military-dressed people. They were dressed in all kinds of uniforms, depending on their rank. The arrival of the higher-ranked military people was preceded by soldiers in parade uniform. Some were holding decorated spears. Each general had six soldiers in parade uniform, holding decorated spears and walking ahead of the general in two rows. The highest ranking general, that was Vas Nu Pieds (as you remember, my dad had promoted him to this position) had also, in addition to the six soldiers four cymbalists, each with a cymbal on each hand, striking their cymbals clankingly.

"A short time after the military generals and their advisers arrived, the audience hall became very quiet. Then the pharaoh's chamberlain opened the door between the room where my dad and I were staying and the audience hall, and he announced the entrance of my dad, the pharaoh. Well, as usual, the generals and all others stood up, and they kneeled and saluted the pharaoh in the manner that was the protocol of the court. And they shouted, 'Long live the pharaoh, our god and master.' My dad instructed them to sit down, which they did.

"My father then opened the session, and here is what he said: 'I thank all of you for being here on such a short notice. I'll talk to you frankly, as you are the upper crust of this country's defense forces.'

"Then he said, 'In different communications I had with the gods, the gods warned me that some enemies were planning to harm me and Egypt. I was also told by the gods that some of those who wanted to harm me and Egypt were not only from the outside but also from within the country, and they may be from the palace itself. I was also warned by the gods to be careful.'

"Then he added, 'Till these conversations with the gods, I felt that Egypt had no need for a strong military because the deserts to the east and west and the Mediterranean to the north protected our country from invasion. As you also know, we do not have any ambitions to conquer other people's lands as we possess the richest lands in the known world.

"'With this information received from the gods, I would like you all to give me frank assessments of the situations at the different frontiers of the country. General Vas Nu Pieds, please introduce each head of the brigades by where they are located alongside the frontiers of the country. Let's start first by the southern frontier, and then the western frontier, and finally with the eastern frontier.'

"'Your Majesty, may you live, prosper, and be healthy,' said Vas Nu Pieds. 'I will let General Suce Mon Pouce, the head of the brigade that is in the south of the country, take the lead and describe the situation there.'

"'Your Majesty, may you live, prosper, and be healthy,' said General Suce Mon Pouce. 'I am your slave and humble servant and would beg your patience in listening to my description of our neighbors of the south. This area comprises lands of several ancient kingdoms and is extremely poor and distressing. The people living there are influenced by the cultural and religious interactions they have with us. For centuries, trade developed between these people and our people. Our caravans carried grain to Kush and returned to Aswan with ivory, incense, hides, and carnelian. As you know, Your Majesty, may you live, prosper, and be healthy, carnelian is the stone that our armed forces prize for arrowheads, but they are also used for jewelry. Our southern governors particularly value the gold we get in Kush.'

"General Suce Mon Pouce took a deep breath then said, 'There, beyond our frontiers of the south that is the land upstream from the First Cataract, is the area called Kush, known today as Nubia. For many years in the past, our soldiers penetrated Kush periodically. Now we have a network of forts along the Nile as far south as Samnah to guard the flow of gold from mines in Wawat, and we have no problems with the population of these areas, except that from time to time, some bandits attempt to rob the caravans traveling between our country and Kush.'

"General Suce Mon Pouce took a deep breath again then said, 'Your Majesty, may you live, prosper, and be healthy. As your slave and humble servant, I can assure you that there is almost no danger for Egypt to be attacked from the south. The bandits who attempt to rob the caravans traveling between our country and Kush are of a small scale and are as much Egyptian bandits as bandits from Kush. They can be handled with a minimum amount of force, mostly a police type of force.'

"Here I have to tell you, Kendall, that what was known then as the kingdom of Kush was more or less the area that we know today as Nubia, in Upper Egypt.

"'Thank you, Suce Mon Pouce,' said my dad. Then he turned to Vas Nu Pieds and asked, 'What is going on in the western frontier?'

"'Your Majesty, may you live, prosper, and be healthy,' said Vas Nu Pieds. 'I will let General Mord Ta Langue, the head of the brigade that is in the western frontier of our country, take the lead and describe to you the situation there.'

"'Your Majesty, may you live, prosper, and be healthy,' said General Mord Ta Langue. 'As your slave and humble servant, I can assure you that there is almost no danger for Egypt to be attacked from the west. The territories west of our country, known as Libya, are inhabited by rude and uncivilized nomadic tribes. These tribes live by eating the flesh of wild animals that they hunt and on the herbage of the soil like our cattle. They have neither customs nor laws. And they do not have any ruler with authority to rule over them. They roam around and do not have fixed habitations. They sleep in shelters they mount at night wherever they happen to be. This area is inhabited with savage lions called Gaetulian lions that are known to tear their prey, human or other, to pieces.'

"General Mord Ta Langue took a deep breath again then said, 'Because of the incoherence and lack of organization of these tribes, as well as the large desert that Egypt has between where these tribes live and the part of our country that is inhabited, Egypt has no need for a strong military in the west. The couple of brigades we have there are more than sufficient to guard this frontier, except for when we train our soldiers there when they are bored and do very little.'

"'Thank you, Mord Ta Langue,' said my dad.

"Then he turned to Vas Nu Pieds and asked him to let him know what was going on in the eastern frontier.

"'Your Majesty, may you live, prosper, and be healthy,' said Vas Nu Pieds. 'I will let General Suce Ta Levre, the head of the brigade that is in the western frontier of our country, take the lead and describe the situation there. General Suce Ta Levre, go ahead and give your report to the pharaoh.'

"General Suce Ta Levre stood up, took a deep breath, and then said, 'Your Majesty, may you live, prosper, and be healthy. Our empire, established by your ancestor, Pharaoh Thutmose III, after the battle of Megiddo, is still pretty much under our control. However, I should tell Your Majesty that we are experiencing some problems in our border with Southern Syria. The king of this country that you defeated and that gave you his daughter as one of your wives is conspiring with other princes, and he is attempting to create an army large enough to seize lands that belong to Egypt on our border. He is creating bonds with the rulers that are vassals to Your Majesty. He is also communicating with all the gods, ours, as well as the ones that Syrians worship, to get their blessing for attacking us. Our spies reveal that although most are refusing to join this new coalition, a few are arming and preparing to invade our sacred country.'

"The pharaoh then asked General Suce Ta Levre, 'Tell me what this prince is plotting. We gave him a very good deal, and I married his daughter. What on earth does he want? Did you find out the real goal of this ingrate?'

"'Your Majesty, may you live, prosper, and be healthy,' said General Suce Ta Levre. 'We are being kept informed by our spies, and it seems that his daughter sent him messages telling him that Egypt is very rich in gold and that it would be easy for him to conquer this country now and get all the riches of Egypt as booty. Anyway, your Majesty—'

"General Suce Ta Levre took a deep breath and then

said, 'We are adding a couple of brigades with their chariots to our forces in this frontier, and we are fortifying our positions to meet and defeat these arrogant and greedy princes. We realize that your wife, the daughter of the organizer of this rebellion, may be a spy herself, or she may be directing spies to help her father. Considering this fact, we are expecting orders from Your Majesty, may you live, prosper, and be healthy, and will do as you wish.'

"After he heard the generals' reports on what was going along the different frontiers of Egypt, and after these generals left the audience hall, the only people that remained with my dad and me were Chamberlain Kar Tu Mow and General Vas Nu Pieds. It was then that my father asked us all to sit down. As you remember, it was normally taboo for these people sit down around the pharaoh in this informal manner. When we all were sitting, my father addressed us, saying, 'I am worried about what the god Amun-Ra told me when we went to see him in his temple during your wedding, General Vas Nu Pieds. You heard these words, didn't you, Khouf? These words still resonate in my head: "Be aware, Amenohotep and Khouf. There is a nest of vipers in the palace. Sohounac may find his way to them and could use the power of his friends to achieve his evil goals." Khouf, my son, the god Amun-Ra does not give such warnings easily.'

"'Listening to the generals' reports, especially the one of General Suce Ta Levre, and remembering the warning of the god Amun-Ra, I feel compelled to take action immediately. Thus I want to follow two courses of action. First, I would like to send a two-person mission to the king of Syria with gifts of gold and silver to see if that would appease him. Chamberlain Kar Tu Mow, tell me who the best negotiators are to carry this mission.'

"'Your Majesty, may you live, prosper, and be healthy,' said Chamberlain Kar Tu Mow. 'I would suggest the two diplomats that were with you when you negotiated the peace treaty with the king of Syria. Remember, Your Majesty, how suave and to the point they were.'

"'Oh yes, Kar Tu Mow, yes. Tut-on-aris and Bon-a-rien are indeed pleasant, tactful, and well-mannered. They know how to deal and negotiate and avoid friction. They are the ones to be sent in my name. Prepare this expedition immediately and give them food and ammunitions, as well as two chariots from the royal chariots.'

"'Your Majesty, may you live, prosper, and be healthy,' said Chamberlain Kar Tu Mow. 'I shall immediately provide them as you ordered, as well as with a couple of speed chariots from Your Majesty's court.'

"'Now, my dear Kar Tu Mow, I would like to go to the temples of Karnak and Luxor immediately with my son to consult with the god Amun-Ra again and visit with other gods there to determine the best set of actions I should take in addressing the situation with our enemies east of our frontier.'

"Then, turning to Chamberlain Kar Tu Mow, he asked, 'Please provide me and my son the fastest means of transportation to go to Karnak and Luxor.'

"'Your Majesty, may you live, prosper, and be healthy,' said Chamberlain Kar Tu Mow. 'I would suggest that you use two of your parade chariots. These chariots have the advantage of always having the right of way, and as Your Majesty knows, the people of Epet (this was the name of the city of Thebes then. This city is what you know as Luxor today) are known for being very undisciplined and for obstructing other people's chariots with their chariots. They will not, however, try to do such a thing with the pharaoh's chariot and the guards surrounding you and your son.' That was what Chamberlain Kar Tu Mow told us.

"Kendall, Kendall, are you listening to me? Tell me, why are you looking at me this way? Why?"

"I don't know what you are talking about. Is what you are telling me correct? From what I remember, you told me before that your dad had a chapel for the god Amun-Ra in the palace. You also told me that he met with and talked to this god several times in this chapel. Is that true? And if it is, then why the hullabaloo for you and him to go to Karnak temple to visit and talk to the god Amun-Ra?"

"Let me explain to you, dear Kendall. We lived in our palace close to the city of what you now call Luxor. This palace was built by one of my ancestors. This city was called Luxor by the Arab invaders. This word in Arabic means 'the palaces.' The city was first named Ipet Sout by my ancestors. This name meant the 'most esteemed of places.' This name, as pronounced by the Egyptians of my time, led the Greek visitors to hear this name and pronounce it as Thebes. Since then, this name was used to identify the city and the temples in it. You should also know that the people of Egypt during my time called their temples the houses of eternity.

"The city of Luxor (Ipet Sout or Thebes) was a pleasant city beside the Nile River. On one side of what was Thebes was the Karnak temple complex, with the so-called temple of Luxor not too far away from it. Close to the other end of the city was my dad's palace.

"Across the river of Thebes was a valley where most of the tombs of the pharaohs, as well as of their wives and of famous princes of this time, were located. Now let me take you back to the temples. There is a reason for being so detailed about all of what is on and around the city of Thebes. This is particularly true for all the temples there and of the area what was the center of a great part of your ancestor's history. Once I finish talking to you, you will realize how important it may be for you to know these facts."

After hearing these words, I went to sleep with Mignonne, my dog, next to me.

8 The Karnak Temple Complex

"My dear princess Kendall, the so-called Karnak temple is not just one temple. It is several temples connected to one another. When most people talk about this temple, they refer to the largest temple of this complex—the temple of the god Amun-Ra. This temple is the largest part of this complex. It is really like a palace—it is the main residence of the god Amun-Ra. I will tell you more about this place in a few moments.

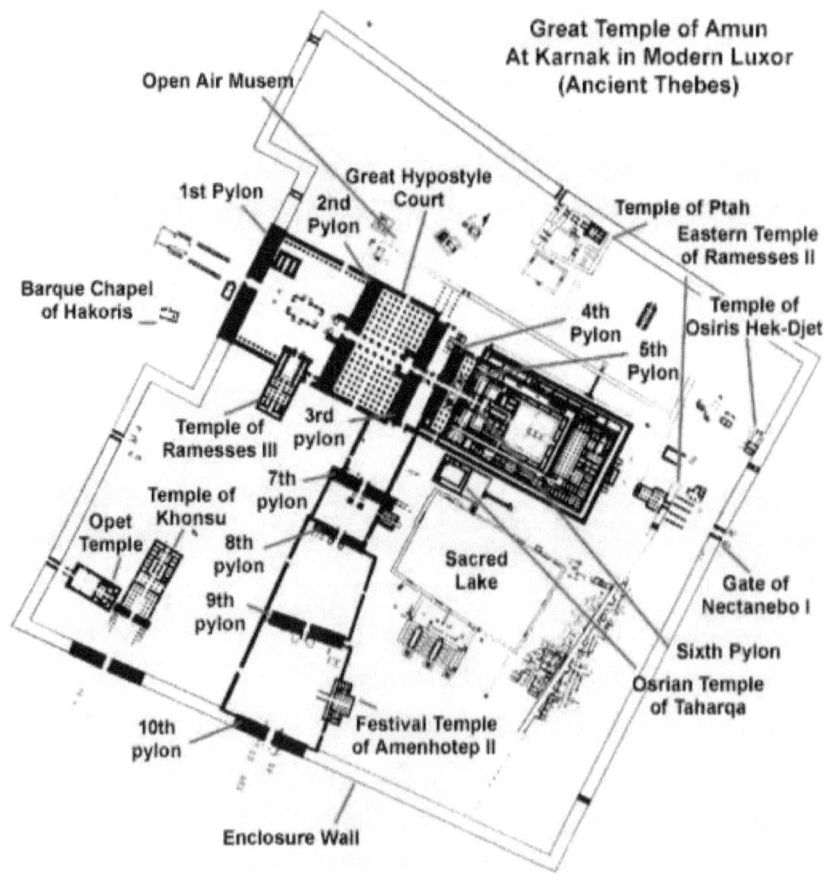

I have a very special interest in giving you detail description of this temple. One is that it is an incredible complex of buildings, and the second is that I know quite a bit about it because one of my teachers was an architect very familiar with the temple details. So when we talk about the Karnack temple we really talk about the temple itself and the complex that surround it. As you can see in the picture of the complex, the temple is the center of the complex, and it is surrounded by a lake and by other smaller buildings.

"There are two smaller temples connected directly to the main temple. One of these temples, located in the south of Amun-Ra's temple, is the temple dedicated to the goddess Mut. This goddess is one of the wives of Amun-Ra. The other temple, located in the north of Amun-Ra's temple, is the temple of the god Montu. Montu is the falcon-headed god of war. If the god Amun-Ra's temple is his palace for when he resides on earth, these two temples would just be small mansions compared to Amun-Ra's temple.

The inserted figure that follows clearly illustrate my explanations. There you have a plan of the main Karnack temple itself. For you to understand the scale of this

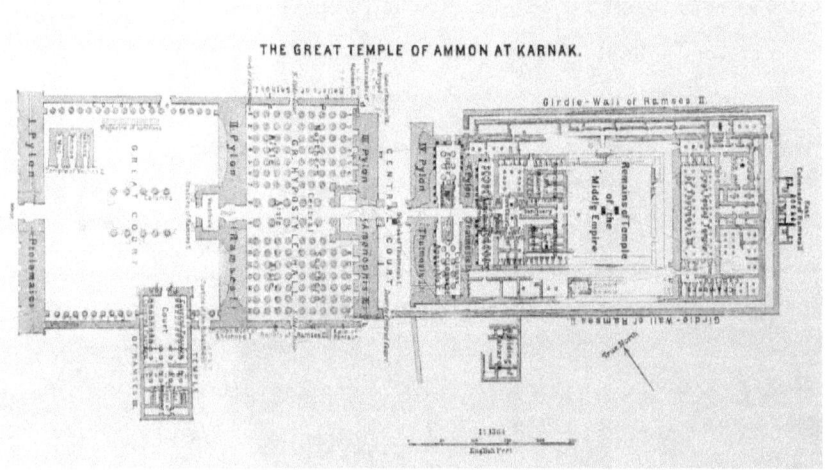

THE GREAT TEMPLE OF AMMON AT KARNAK.

temple, imagine being in a church cathedral, a very large cathedral and multiply by three or four time the size of this cathedral: there you may imagine the size of the temple itself. The temple appears in bold lines in the so-called temple complex. This complex has the size of a city, and in fact it is a city, a self-sufficient city.

"The construction of the Karnak complex started some four thousand years ago by the Egyptian pharaoh Wah-ankh Intef. This ruler erected an eight-sided sandstone column to the god Amun-Ra. The inscriptions on this column said that he made this monument for that god.

"If you were there, Kendall, you would see that behind the high walls surrounding the complex were gold-topped obelisks which pierced the sky. Also in the complex are shrines, smaller temples, columns, and statues worked with gold, electrum, and precious stones such as lapis lazuli that are shining.

"A better view of this complex as a whole is the bird's-eye-view of this complex. There you could better imagine how this site is crowded with buildings and other constructions. This rendering would help you imagine the beauty and grandeur of this temple complex. Also the

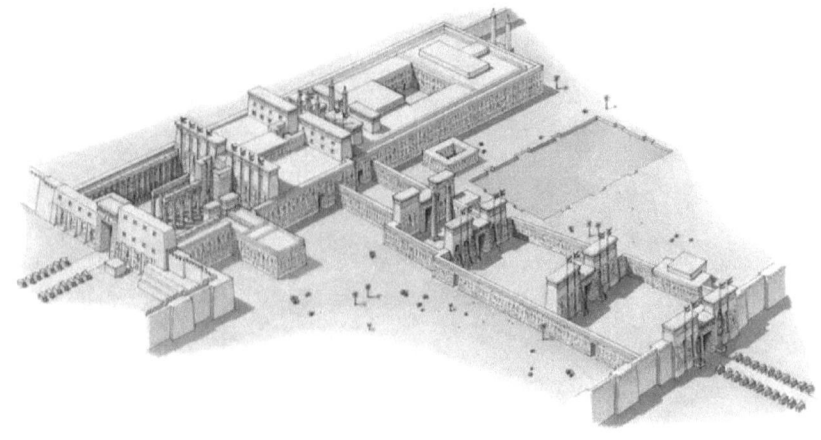

picture of columns supporting part of the roof show the fabulous richness of the decoration of this temple.

"The Karnak complex can be divided into four areas. To the north, a large enclosure is home to the temple of the god Montu. The other enclosure is dedicated to the goddess Ma'at. There are also numerous smaller buildings of stone and mudbrick. The Montu temple may have been connected by an avenue of sphinxes to a much earlier temple for the same Montu god at Medamud, a site that is located five kilometers (three miles) farther north. To the east side, Amenhotep IV or Akhenaten built a huge open-air temple complex dedicated to his solar deity—the Aten. To the south, another enclosure wall surrounds a temple to the goddess Mut and other smaller temples for Amenhotep III and Rameses III. None of these temples are now open to tourists.

"The fourth area is the largest and most important. It's called the central en-closure. This is the area where the great Temple of Amun-Ra, king of the gods, is. And it is where the pharaoh wants to come and converse with the god Amun-Ra. This building alone stretches 1,220 feet (375 meters) front to back and covers over 61 acres (25 hect-ares). The central enclo-sure covers 247 acres (100 hectares), and in

addition to the Temple of Amen, this enclosure encompasses temples to Ptah, Khonsu, Osiris, Opet, and others. Surrounding the four temple areas, buried under several yards of Nile silt, the remains of ancient Thebes extend outward in a huge urban sprawl that probably covers thousands of hectares.

"You should know, Kendall, that my ancestors who lived during the New Kingdom were exuberant builders, and they spent fortunes adding new buildings or extending existing ones in the temple of Karnak. These extended the temple size and complexity, as well as adding to its wealth. The priests of the temple of Amun-Ra were the richest people in Egypt. The records of this temple show that the priests of the temple of Amun-Ra owned over 81,000 slaves and servants, 421,000 head of cattle, 691,000 acres of agricultural land, 83 ships, 46 shipyards, and 65 cities." "Wow, that is quite a lot, Khouf. So my ancestors were great builders and spent a lot of money for buildings."

"Yes, they were. When Rameses III was the pharaoh, he gave as gifts to the temple 31,833 kilograms of gold, 997,805 kilograms of silver, 2,395,120 kilograms of copper, 3,722 bolts of cloth, 880,000 bushels of wheat, 289,530 ducks and geese, and untold quantities of oil, wine, fruits, and vegetables. All this wealth made Amun-Ra the richest god of the antiquity and made this god truly the king of the gods. Many structures were built in his honor. Over two hundred large structures have been found there.

"Undoubtedly, there were hundreds more. Some of these structures were simple mudbrick buildings that have nearly vanished. Some were elegant structures built

of fine alabaster. Many others were enormous monuments of sandstone and granite with walls 15 meters (49 feet) thick that stand 50 meters (164 feet) high. All these structures made Karnak so crowded that new structures were built wherever space permitted, and older buildings were often demolished to accommodate the new structures. With this chaos, it was evident that Karnak temple never followed a master plan for its site.

"At such time, the city of Thebes had a population of over fifty thousand people. And up to this day, this ancient city is still virtually unexplored by archaeologists.

"Oops, Kendall, I should have told you about the other important temples of Thebes. There is the so-called Amenhotep III Temple. This is another large ancient Egyptian temple complex located on the west bank of the River Nile. This temple was built by my dad's ancestor. It was not only the largest temple built in Thebes but was also larger than the temple of Amun-Ra at Karnak. It measured 700 by 550 meters. It covered 385,000 square meters (4,200,000 square feet). The only remains of this temple are the two statues that were in front of it—the Colossi of Memnon" that you see next to this text.

"So many temples in such a small area. With such large areas of desert, why did they not use some of these areas?"

"I don't know, Kendall. I was just a small boy then. It is too late to ask our ancestors why they did not."

"Ha ha ha, right you are."

"There is also the Luxor Temple dedicated to the Theban Triad of Amun-Ra, Mut, and Chons. This temple shown across this text was built during the New Kingdom, the focus of the annual Opet Festival in which a cult statue of Amun was paraded down the Nile from nearby Karnak temple (ipet-isut) to stay there for a while with his consort Mut in a celebration of fertility.

"Kendall, I will back up from my description of events

to describe for a little bit the location of the different temples related to where the statue of the god Amun-Ra was located. Before reaching the so-called Karnak temple, you have to go by the Luxor Temple. This temple, as I described earlier to

you, was located on the east bank of the River Nile in the city known as Luxor today, which was the city of Thebes then. It was founded in 1400 BCE. Thebes was known in the Egyptian language as *ipet resyt*, or 'the southern sanctuary.'"

"So Luxor and Thebes are one and the same, but with different names."

"Yes, Kendall, and Luxor Temple was dedicated to the Theban Triad of Amun-Ra, Mut, and Chons and was built during the New Kingdom. This temple was the focus of the annual Opet Festival. During this festival, a cult statue of Amun-Ra was paraded down the Nile from the Luxor Temple to nearby Karnak temple (the Ipet-isut Temple). At the end of the parade, the statue of Amun-Ra was to stay there for a while, with the statue of the goddess Mut, in a celebration of fertility (hence its name). The Luxor Temple and the Karnack temple were connected."

"You mean to say that the Luxor Temple was connected with the group of temples that constituted the Karnack temple?"

"Yes, Kendall. The earliest parts of the Luxor Temple are still standing. The lodge of the "Barque Chapel" is just behind the first pylon. It was built by the pharaoh Hatshepsut and appropriated by the pharaoh Tuthmosis III. The main parts of the temple—the colonnade and the sun court—were built by the pharaoh Amenhotep III and had a later addition built by the pharaoh Rameses II. This pharaoh also built the entrance pylon and the two obelisks that linked the Hatshepsut buildings with the main temple."

"Are these obelisks still there?"

"No, Kendall. One of these two obelisks was taken to France and is now at the center of the Place de la Concorde. You should also know that to the rear of the Luxor Temple are chapels that were built by Tuthmosis III."

"OK."

"Let's go back to the temple of Karnack. This temple had two axes—one that went north to south and the other that extended east to west. The southern axis continued toward Luxor Temple. An avenue of ram-headed sphinxes along this axis connected the two temples. This was the avenue we took—my father and I—to go to visit with the god Amun-Ra. The enclosed picture shows you how this avenue looked like."

"This avenue looks like wow. Is every one of these sphinx hand carved in stone as they seem to be?"

"Yes, Kendall, they were hand carved in stone."

"Wow, that's quite some work."

"We finally arrived at the Karnack temple. This was in the very large enclosed open space. As I told you before, in this space was a temple for the god Montu. Another small enclosure within the open space was dedicated to the goddess Ma'at. And there were numerous smaller buildings of stone and mudbrick within the large enclosure temple to the goddess Mut and smaller temples for Amenhotep III and Rameses III.

"Kendall, it will not be long before I will disappear from your life, and all that I am telling you will be like a dream for you. You should always remember this dream because it shall be like a master plan for you. That is, if you decide when you get older to become an Egyptologist."

"What? What do you mean? And how does that fit in the descriptions you are giving me?"

"This is the first time I am being so blunt about telling you my best wish for your future. You are an Egyptian princess of royal blood by your dad, and the few secrets I have and will give you in my talks will make you discover the incredible wealth of your ancestors. And because of your kindness to me, you will become one of the most famous Egyptologists in history. Stop looking at me that way. I know what I am telling you, and you shall make it happen.

"Let's go back now to the purpose of my dad's visit with the god Amun-Ra. As I told you before the long description of Karnak and Thebes, he wanted to consult with this god on the best course to take with the situation that was created in the country by Egypt's eastern neighbors."

"Yes, I remember that this was the main objective, if not the only one for this trip."

"As we arrived near the Karnack temple, we realized that there was a commotion taking place inside the complex. It seemed that the chamberlain sent a messenger ahead of us to notify the grand priest of the pharaoh's visit. Thus the temple personnel were preparing to receive us with pomp and circumstances."

"Well, your dad was the pharaoh. Therefore they had to receive him with pomp and circumstances. It is very normal."

"As we got to the entrance of the temple complex, we found a committee of the temple's most important priests, headed by the grand priest, waiting for us.

Other priests and personnel were standing on the two sides of the main passage in the temple. There were musicians playing their instruments. And they were playing hymns that welcomed my dad, the pharaoh, as well as me. And as we were entering the perimeter of the temple, the grand priest came ahead and knelt in front of us and gave us a tirade.

"'Welcome to the holy temple of Karnack, Your Majesty, god Horus on earth. May you live, prosper, and be healthy. Also welcome to your son, who shall succeed you to the throne after a healthy and long life of Your Majesty. Welcome, the two of you, in the name of the god Amun-Ra, as well as in the names of all the gods of the temple.'

"As the grand priest knelt, the temple's most important priests and members of the reception committee that were waiting for us, as well as the other priests and personnel that were standing on the two sides of the main passage in the temple, also knelt, chanting the glory of my father, the pharaoh, and wishing him a long and blessed life.

"My dad invited the grand priest and the receiving committee to stand up, and he gestured to the crowds on the two sides of the passage to also stand up. The grand priest and the receiving committee stood up, came to us, and bowed to the pharaoh as if wanting to kiss his feet. My dad immediately gestured, asking them to stand up again, and he started conversing with the grand priest. He told him the purpose of his visit and asked him if he could arrange a meeting for the two of us with the god Amun-Ra in his sacred place.

"'I will try,' the grand priest said. 'For you, milord, it will be no problem, as you are a living god. I hope that it will also be OK for Your Majesty's son.'

"The grand priest then invited us to join him and directed us toward an area where they prepared to serve a majestic meal. But what was in front of us was a large rectangle of about twelve-by-eighteen-feet, framed with a low curb. This rectangle was filled with sand, and at the center of the long side of the rectangle was a large table made of stone. Soon after we sat down, we saw six men bringing a bull toward the rectangle. The bull was enormous and was very excited. Two of these men were holding the bull's head with a thick rope. Two other men were holding the body of the bull with ropes too. These ropes were holding the bull around his waist, close to his front legs, and two other men were holding the bull around his waist, close to his back legs.

"These men brought the bull in the sanded area in front of us. The grand priest recited some prayer. Then with a large tool that looked almost like a hammer, he strongly hit the bull on the head. The bull, for a moment, looked totally lost. That was the moment the temple butcher sliced the bull's neck with a sharp butcher knife. He did it right there in front of us. When a sufficient amount of blood drained in the sand, the six men moved the body of the bull to the marble table. The butcher then proceeded to cut the bull's body in pieces. Some of these pieces were offered to the god Amun-Ra, moved to where the statue was, and burned in front of his statue. The best pieces after that were cooked and offered to us

with lots of other goodies.

"This majestic and ceremonial meal took place when musicians were playing their instruments and dancers were dancing to entertain us. My father then offered to the grand priest the customary gift of gold incense, myrrh, and labdanum. The gold was for the maintenance of the temple. The incense, myrrh, and the labdanum were to be used during the ceremonies around the god's statue. The dinner ended with a series of entertainments, music, dancers, and poetry recitals, all in the honor of the gods and the pharaoh.

We were then directed to the sleeping quarters of the temple, despite our hopes of returning back to our palace. Naturally, that was because the main purpose of our visit was to seek the advice of the god Amun-Ra, and that was not possible before the next morning.

"Kendall, I am sure that you will understand why I hardly slept the whole night. All the pump and the killing of this poor bull, and all the hullabaloo that took place at the temple."

"Yikes, yes, I do. I can't stand seeing so much blood."

"Early in the morning, Kendall, I heard all kinds of songs and loud prayers. Then the music came close to where we were sleeping, and I understood that was probably a wake-up call. And it was."

"It's nice to be awakened with nice music."

"Yes. And to have breakfast in bed. Breakfast was brought up to us very discreetly when we were still in bed, and six lovely young girls in dancing attires came with the breakfast to entertain us. They were very pretty and looked very sweet, almost as sweet as my friend Mange Ta Soupe. They brought ablutions and, after the breakfast, helped us with our morning grooming. When this was over, they left discreetly.

"Then the grand priest came and knocked on our door. We invited him in. He asked us how we slept and if the accommodations were suitable. We had a short pleasant conversation, and he told us to let him know when we would be ready to go to the god Amun-Ra. We were ready. He then directed us toward the exit of where we were.

"As soon as he opened the door of our sleeping accommodations, the music started playing loud hymns to the glory and long life of the pharaoh and his family. There was a big band of musicians and several dancing girls. Among them were the six lovely young girls in dancing attire that came with the breakfast to entertain us."

"Nice."

"They were all smiles and were eying me intensely. I felt intimidated and I blushed. There were two chaises, each to sit two people. In one of these two chairs was a little boy, maybe eight or nine years old, dressed in gold. Everything he was wearing was in pure twenty-four-karat gold. All his clothes, his hat, and the decoration on his clothes were all in gold. He was almost like one of the statues erected in the temple, except that he was very much alive. He greeted us as a subject greets his king, when this king was also a god. He bowed all the way to the floor and, with a child's voice, almost as a girl's voice, said all the words he was taught to address a pharaoh with a facility and a fluency that was extraordinary for a child of his age.

"As we were climbing on our chairs, I dared to ask the grand priest, 'Who is this boy? Is he your son?'

"The grand priest answered me with a big smile on his face. 'No, Your Highness. He is the "voice," as you will soon see.'

"Once the three of us were sitting in our respective chaises, the procession started to move.

"As the procession was at a short stop next to a right turn, I was close to the boy. I could not help but turn around in my chair and ask the golden boy, 'What is your name?'

"He was very polite in responding to me. He told me, 'I am the voice, Your Highness.'

"The voice's voice was that of a very young boy, almost like the voice of a girl. That left me very puzzled. What's a name for a boy? And what's a way to have him dressed?

"Let's go back to the procession. I kept being puzzled by the very young golden boy. I was asking myself what was so special about his voice to be named the voice. When he answered me, his voice had nothing special. It was normal for his age to have a voice like the voice of a girl. As I was still day-dreaming about this boy's voice, I realized that we were almost at the loca-tion of the god Amun-Ra's alcove in the majestic temple. As we arrived at the entrance of the god Amun-Ra's alcove, the grand priest asked us to wait at the entrance outside of the alcove as he entered there with the

THE BOY NAMED THE VOICE

young golden boy. From the outside, we could see the inside of the alcove.

"Kendall, right in front of us was the statue of the god. It was tall and majestic. It was carved from precious white marble and almost looked like a mirror, so brilliant it was.

He had a head of a ram, and his head was of pure gold. This was the king of the gods. He was the god of the wind as well as the god of the sun, which was what the letters *Ra* meant in *Amun-Ra*. The statue was lightly painted here and there to emphasize certain aspects of the statue. Believe me, Kendall. Even now as I talk to you, even just imagining the statue of the god, I am still impressed.

"In front of the statue was a short column that was about three feet high. The column was made of the precious stone lapis lazuli. At the top of the column was a pure gold sphere of about the same diameter as the column. On the side of the alcove, we could detect a much smaller statue of the goddess Amunet. Amunet was the wife of Amun-Ra and was one of the creation goddesses. My dad and I were observing all these as we were out of the alcove, waiting to be invited in.

"Soon we were invited in by the grand priest. The grand priest ceremoniously introduced us to the god. The voice was standing near the small column. As soon as the voice put his hand on top of the gold sphere, the earth started to tremble, and small lightning was getting out of the small lapis lazuli column and of the gold sphere. It sounded like thunder was filling the alcove. We felt like we were in the center of a storm, but without any rain. It was frightening. That was when the grand priest asked my father to reintroduce himself and to introduce me.

"Before my dad could talk, the god talked. It was

strange since the god was a statue. But it was the voice
that talked for him. Then I knew why they called him
the voice. When he was talking there, his voice was that
of an old, mature man who was very sure of himself. It
was hard to believe that this voice was coming from the
mouth of this young boy.

"'Amenhotep, I know who you are, and I know that this
young boy is your son. And he is destined to be the next
pharaoh. Now tell me, what brings you here?'

"'Your Holiness, king of all the gods, god of the wind
and god of the sun, I came to ask your advice on a matter
of great importance for our country. My spies are telling me that the small kingdoms east of our country are
preparing to attack Egypt. They may also have their own
spies here in Egypt that are informing them about our
situation. What would your advice be? Should I go and attack them now, or should I wait for them at the frontier?'

"The voice of the god Amun-Ra came out of the boy's
mouth and said, 'Amenhotep, living incarnation of Horus,
I want to help you in this matter, but there is a great and
imminent danger you have to deal with first and immediately. You must be very careful about Sohounac. He is still
alive, and he knows by now what I did for you and for Vas
Nu Pieds's protector, Old Man River. Sohounac is a very
mean creature. He has no power over my word, but he is
a very revengeful person. Now that he knows what I did
for you and Old Man River, he will be after your family
and your descendants. He may not directly reach you, but
he befriended several wicked gods that won't hesitate to
harm you and your family.'

"Then the voice of the god Amun-Ra addressed me
and said, 'Khouf, be careful in your life. You may not know

it, but you are surrounded by evil creatures that want to harm you. Neither you nor pharaoh Amenhotep are aware of who they are. Be aware. There is a nest of vipers in the palace. Do you hear me, Amenhotep and Khouf? Sohounac may find his way to them and could use the power of his friends, the wicked gods, to achieve his evil goals. As to the advice you are asking me to give you, this would be to solve first the situation that surrounds you here and now, then evaluate the situation in the east again when the ambassadors you sent to the kings in the east will come back with more relevant information. In any case, your army should be ready for any situations.'

"Then my dad answered the god. He said, 'Your Holiness, king of all the gods, god of the wind and god of the sun, I thank you for the wise advice you have given me.'

"Then the grand priest, turning toward my dad, said, 'Your Majesty, may you live, prosper, and be healthy. And may the gods give you a long life. I think it is time to leave.'

"Then the god Amun-Ra, via the voice, said, 'Good luck, Amenhotep, and be careful.'

"The grand priest, addressing himself to the god Amun-Ra, said, 'Your Holiness, king of all the gods, god of the wind and god of the sun, I thank you for seeing us and for the advice given to the pharaoh Amenhotep.'

"Then the grand priest, followed by the voice, proceeded to leave the god's alcove. My dad and I followed them.

"Kendall, I will never forget this encounter. It ended up changing my dad's life as well as mine, as you will see when I continue telling you what horrible things happened."

"Oh, poor you. Was it then that you changed into a

frog?" said Kendall.

"No, just be patient, because what happened after is really horrible and very difficult to believe."

"Please tell me, Khouf," insisted Kendall.

"OK, that will come in a few moments. Just be patient.

"We were back in our chariot, and we proceeded to drive it back home to the palace. Because our chariot was so spectacular, we could not speed discreetly through the streets of Thebes. Everybody in our way knew that our chariot was the pharaoh's, and they deduced that the two people on it must be the pharaoh and his son. Therefore, many people would kneel in respect, and the other chariots, which were much more modest, would stop and give way to our chariot. The result was quite a bit of a mess. We had to go much slower, and we even sometimes stopped. It was a complete mess, and we were causing it. As we were advancing slowly within the mess we were producing, we got to another spot that was also a complete mess.

"Traffic coming the other way also completely stopped, and that was for as long as we could see. Slowly, and losing lots of time, we were advancing toward our palace. The traffic going the other direction started also to move toward the temple. That was when we realized the cause of the two traffic messes. Another palace chariot was directing itself toward the temple. When the two chariots finally were across each other, we understood the why of this situation. The other chariot was driven by the pharaoh's chamberlain. The two chariots stopped, and it was then that we realized that the chamberlain was coming to give the pharaoh an important message. For a long few minutes, the chamberlain greeted my dad as was required by saying, 'May Your Majesty live a long life, prosper, and be healthy. I have important news to give you.'

"'Fine,' said my dad. 'Tell me what they are.'

"'Two messengers came from the king of Syria with two large black-and-gold urns that, according to them, contain gifts for you, Your Majesty. When I asked them about the two messengers you sent to this king, their answer was that it is contained in the two urns among the gifts he sent you. They disembarked the two urns in the palace court between your residence and the official part of the palace. I offered them a place to stay until your return, but they excused themselves, telling me that they were instructed by the king of Syria to return immediately after delivering the two urns with their messages inside them. We kept insisting that at least they get a meal or refreshments before leaving, but they were really in a hurry to go. And they left immediately.'"

9 The Assasination of My Father

"'As soon as they left, we looked at the two urns well,' said the chamberlain. They were really beautiful. The wood was black Syrian ebony. Its upper parts were covered with sheets of twenty-four-karat gold. They had faces of the death gods, and these faces were also in black ebony. The eyes in these urns were made of precious stones. Each of the two urns was composed of two parts. What I was describing to you, Your Majesty, may god give you a long life and good health, was the upper part of the urns. The lower part was as beautiful, also all in black Syrian ebony and uncrustier of gold leaves, silver, and semiprecious stones.

"'OK, OK,' said my dad. 'We shall see what the precious stuff you are talking about ounce at the palace.'

"My dad thanked the chamberlain, and we continued our way to the palace. It took us quite a bit of time to get there, but we finally made it. My dad decided to go home first get refreshed, and he had me do the same. And after we did so and had a meal, we decided to go and see the king of Syria's gifts. We discussed why these messengers were so much in a hurry to leave without reaching any conclusion. We even kind of asked ourselves how to thank him and reciprocate.

"We entered the palace court, and the two urns were there where the chamberlain told us they were.

"'Wow,' said my dad, 'what on earth is that?'

"The chamberlain, who was expecting us, told my dad, 'Your Majesty, these jars were placed there, but I will have them moved to an adequate place with a carpet under them, just in case they contain pieces of jewelry.'

"He also said, 'When Your Majesty shall be ready to see what's in them, I will place seats and will invite other members of his court to join us.'

"My dad and I went to refresh ourselves and have a nap. During this time, things were being done in the court. The chamberlain chose a more adequate location for placing the urns. He had them there and had a carpet placed under them.

Then he had a couple of dozen chairs brought there and located in a form of an amphitheater around these two urns. Naturally, in the center of this arrangement, there were two armchairs with ornaments that had to be used by my dad and me. It was late when we got up from our nap, so we decided to look at the urns the next day in the morning. The chamberlain invited the people that had to join us, and the next morning when we came to the urns, everyone was there. They immediately stood up and bowed to my dad and me (I guess). Once my dad sat

down, he invited the whole audience to also sit down.

"My dad then asked the chamberlain, who was acting as a master of ceremony, to uncover the first urn. The chamberlain, who was seated closest to the urn, stood up and went to uncover the urn as instructed. As soon as the urn's cover was removed, a big *ahhhhh* came out of everybody's mouth. A head of a man was there, right at the top and under the cover of the urn. My dad shouted, 'This is the head of Ambassador Tut-On-Aris! Oh, what a cursed king this is. Cover this urn and open the other, Chamberlain Kar Tu Mow.'

"'Yes, Your Majesty. May you have a long life in good health.'

"Kendall, the whole audience was breathless, waiting for the chamberlain to uncover the other urn. So he did. And as soon as the urn was uncovered, another big *ahhhhh* came out of everybody's mouths.

"Another head of a man was there, right at the top and under the cover of the urn. My dad shouted, 'For heaven's sake, this is the head of Ambassador Bon-a-rien!'

"Again he instructed Chamberlain Kar Tu Mow to cover the urn. He was furious, very much so. He then addressed himself to the palace grand priest and asked him to give a funeral of a prince to these two ambassadors.

"My dad then addressed himself to Vas Nu Pieds and told him, 'General Vas Nu Pieds, I want you to prepare to invade Syria and to give this nasty king a good lesson.'

"After that, he turned to his Syrian wife and asked her, 'Did you know what your dad was going to do?'

"She blushed and swore that she did not know. His son by her, however, intervened, saying, 'Didn't your father tell you that he would come and visit you soon, Mother?'

"She blushed and said, 'I do not remember anything like that. Shut up, son.'

"Dad was furious. He remembered what the god Amun-Ra told him about being surrounded with serpents. He then asked the grand priest and his assistant, 'Please have the heads of the two assassinated ambassadors removed, and have them embalmed.'

"He also asked Vas Nu Pieds, 'General Vas Nu Pieds, look on how we can get the rest of the bodies of these two unlucky ambassadors.'

"Vas Nu Pieds answered the

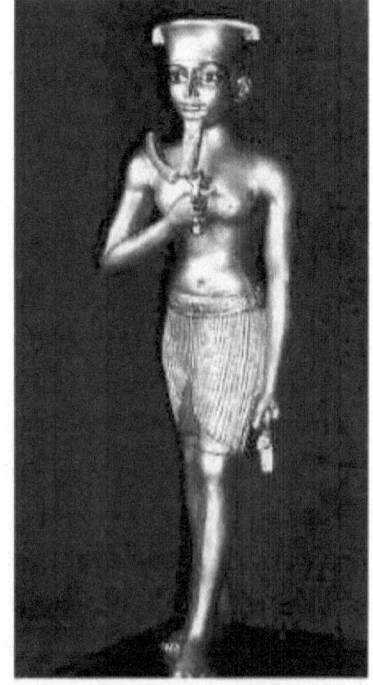

THE SUN GOD AMUN RA

pharaoh, 'I shall do my best to do so, Your Majesty.'

"By then, the two heads were removed, so my dad stood up and went to look at what was inside one of the urns. He looked in the urn. It was kind of dark, so he leaned his head more toward the urn. Suddenly he shouted, taking his head away from the urn. And as he was doing it, we all saw two mini jets going into his eyes. He was jumping in pain after being blinded was and shouting like I never heard him shout before.

As he was jumping, he hit the urn, and the urn fell on the floor. Suddenly, a cobra snake came out of it and bit my dad in his neck. My poor dad continued jumping for a minute or so and then fell on the floor, still moving like a beheaded chicken.

"Simultaneously, all who were seated immediately ran away from the area as several snakes were getting out of the urn. Only Vas Nu Pieds and I directed ourselves toward my dad. I took my dad in my arms and pulled him away from the snakes as Vas Nu Pieds used a stick to push them away. He asked one of the military men there to get a few swords and sabers as he kept pushing away the snakes.

"My dad was now in the hands of the priests who realized that he was already dead. I turned to them and asked, 'What can we do to bring him back to life?'

"They answered me with 'May Your Majesty live a long life, prosper, and be healthy. Your dad is dead in this world, and he is joining the gods in the other world.'

"It was then that I realized that this was it. From then on, I had to take over as the new pharaoh, or so I thought, as you already know.

"General Vas Nu Pieds, by then, got his swords and,

helped by his upper military assistants, started to kill the snakes that left the urn. As to the other urn, it was immediately covered and taken away to dispose of the snakes inside it.

"Once all the snakes were killed, the general and his assistants left and went to their headquarters to determine what to do next in this situation. The priests took my dad's body, saying the prayers of the dead. He gave my dad's body to the embalmers. Despite the fact that the priest referred to me as the new pharaoh, I was too young to be immediately named as the new pharaoh. A tribunal of gods should have named a tutor. Remember when you asked me what a tutor was, Kendall?"

"Yes, I do."

"And I told you that a tutor is person who would take care of my education and welfare until I would be of age to officially claim the kingship of Egypt and become the new pharaoh. The tutor was supposed to prepare me to be a good pharaoh. Instead of having the tribunal of gods name the tutor who would govern in my name, the Syrian god Baal and the Syrian goddess Reshep did so. They named the tutor and advised the gods of the tribunal of gods that they acted on their behalf in naming the tutor who would take care of my education. It is important for me to tell you that these two Syrian gods were also a sorcerer and a witch.

"Merdonice, the Syrian wife of my dad, was among the people who witnessed the opening of the urns from where the snakes that killed my dad came out. She immediately left the premises to meet with her group of sorcerers and friends. There, after consulting with them, she claimed that her son, my half-brother, was to become the new pharaoh. This, in principle, was impossible, since the boy's mother was not of Egyptian birth, and the pharaoh, at this time, had to have an Egyptian-born father and mother. My tutor, who was a friend of Merdonice, did not take a stand at this. And even if he did, the matter was already approved by the council of gods.

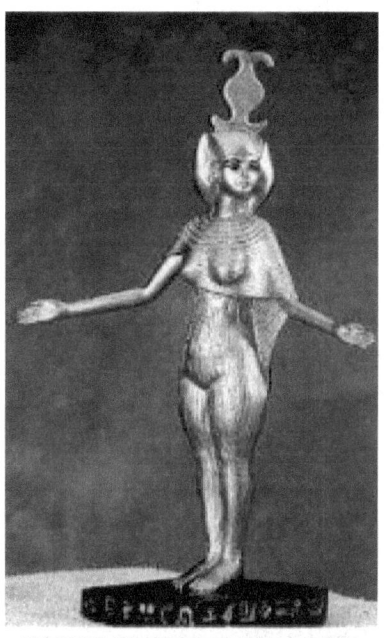

PICTURE OF THE GODDESS NEITH

"Remember I said earlier that a tribunal of gods named my tutor? That was not exactly true. Two gods did so and then gained the approvals of the council of gods. You may compare the gods who were part of the council of gods to the saints and angels of the Christian religion that you practice now. Some of these gods were more powerful than others. Some were good gods, and others were bad gods. The bad gods then were pretty much as wicked as the devil Satan, also known as Lucifer. Most of these gods, good and bad, would take the form of living beings, human or animals, and would talk to people and intervene in their lives.

PICTURE OD AN EGYPTIAN ROYAL CARTOUCHE

"When my dad died, he

joined the gods of Egypt, and my mom immediately claimed the kingship for me, as it was customary to do so. She put that claim to a tribunal of the major gods. This tribunal was presided by the sun god Amun-Ra of the city of Heliopolis.

"Thoth, the god of wisdom, told the sun god Amun-Ra that I should immediately have the Sacred Eye, which was the symbol of the cosmic order of justice and of kingship.

"As I told you earlier, every pharaoh or pharaoh-to-be must receive the Sacred Eye to be considered a pharaoh. The god Shu urged the immediate approval of me

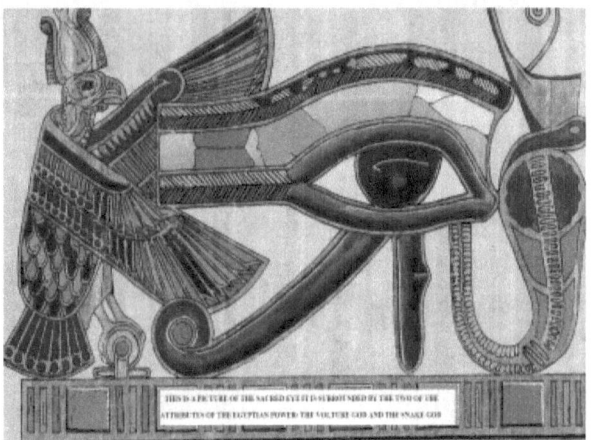

becoming the next pharaoh. The god of wisdom, Thoth, confirmed that approving me as the next pharaoh was a million times right. Immediately, everybody in the pharaoh's palace became very happy.

"But the god Amun-Ra with whom we consulted earlier stopped this happiness short. For some reason, he declared that he did not agree that I should possess the royal name ring—the cartouche. Again, Kendall, as I told you earlier, the cartouche was, in ancient Egypt, the coat of arms that every pharaoh must have.

"The god Amun-Ra suggested that I should go out and have a hand-to-hand fight with my half- brother, the son of Merdonice, the foreign princess that my father married. Most gods were not impressed and preferred very much that I be named the next pharaoh. It appeared later that the god Amun-Ra was very much manipulated by the foreign princess and her entourage of sorcerers and witches who wanted to trick the gods into naming my half-brother the pharaoh. This was despite the fact that almost everyone in the palace knew that this boy was not my father's son and that he was considered my half-brother out of my father's generosity.

"The council of gods decided then to end the discussion by sending a letter to the great creator goddess, Neith, to seek her advice. Goddess Neith replied in no uncertain terms that I should become the pharaoh. She also suggested that some gifts be given to the Syrian god Baal and the Syrian goddess Reshep. These two were also a sorcerer and a witch.

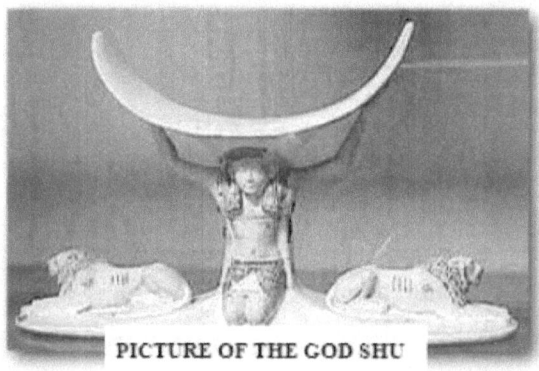

PICTURE OF THE GOD SHU

"The god Baal and the goddess Reshep did not want to accept this decision and refused any gifts from me. The Syrian god Baal personally dared me to go and have a hand fight with my half-brother. I was so offended in my pride that I wanted to fight and show that I could and would win any fight since all the council gods, except the god Baal and the Syrian goddess Reshep, were with me, backing me. Was I wrong, Kendall?

"I went out for the fight without knowing that the Syrian god Baal took the form of a body that looked exactly like my half-brother. We started the fight, and it seemed that I was about to win. It was then that the god Baal used his magic illegally, and I found myself slowly being transformed into a frog. You can imagine how furious I was. The spell was taking hold, and there was nothing I could do to change that. The other gods did not know what happened to me. And even if they knew, it was too late for them to undo the spell.

"Once assured of his victory and his control, the god Baal wanted to supposedly appear nice and assured me that every one hundred years, I would have the opportunity to become human again for a few days at a time. That is, if a beautiful Egyptian princess would kiss me. And she would have to do that without knowing who I was. That way, when I become human again, I can die normally and rejoin my fathers and all the pharaohs of my dynasty in the eternal life.

PICTURE OF THE SYRIAN GOD BAAL

"Then the god Baal returned to the council of gods and told them that it was too late for me to become the pharaoh, as I was killed in a fight in the forest and that a lion ate me. He lied and said that when he arrived to try to save me, I was gone as a meal for the lion and the lion's family. He was a real hypocrite. What he wanted to do was to appear that he was sorry for what happened to me. That was the way the imposter son of my father's Syrian wife became the pharaoh, and I had to wander for thirty centuries as a frog from one generation of frogs to another."

10 The Embalmment of My Dad

THE EMBALMER'S SERVICES

"I know this subject is not the most pleasant to deal with, Kendall, but it is part of life. It is part of our lives here in the pharaonic times. When a person dies, they are brought to the embalmers. And in the case of my dad, the grand priests that were present when my dad was killed by a snakebite immediately carried my dad's body to the embalming building."

"I understand how it must have been very hard for you."

"Yes, it was. Once the body was in the building, the embalmers offered to the family of the deceased three types of services. The best and most expensive kind was said to represent Osiris. The next best was somewhat inferior and cheaper, while the third was the cheapest of all. The grieving family was asked to choose which service they preferred, and their answer was extremely important not only for the deceased but also for themselves. If the family could afford the best service and yet choose not to purchase it, they ran the risk of a haunting. The dead person would know they had been given a cheaper service than they deserved and would not be able to peacefully go into the afterlife. Instead, they would return to make their relatives' lives miserable until the wrong was righted."

"It is so sad to have to do this when a dear one dies."

"Yes, naturally, my mom and I chose the best and most expensive service for my dad. This was done despite my half-brother and his mom's objections. They wanted to choose a less expensive service. This was done when I still had a human body.

"My sweet and dearest Kendall, burial practice and mortuary rituals in ancient Egypt were very serious matters because of our belief that death was not the end of life. A dead person would see and hear what was going around his body, and if wronged, would manage to take revenge with the blessing of the gods. Because the type of burial we chose, they would lay the body of my dad in a special gurney, and it would be the grand priest that would embalm my dad. My mom and I were convinced that we would choose the best kind of coffin where my dad would be buried in, as well as the best funerary rites available and the best treatment of my dad's body. All that I knew as I was still a human being."

"When I became a frog, I found myself in the middle of nowhere, not knowing what to do. I knew pretty soon that I could be in many places without being noticed.

So out of curiosity and of concern about what was being done to my dad, I oriented myself toward the location where the mummification was taking place.

"Yes, Kendall, I entered the building and found myself in a large room where lots of activities were taking place, and most activities were around gurneys, or if you pre-

fer, you may call these gurneys beds. Most beds were very simple like the one shown in the first inserted picture entitled 'Picture showing an embalmer at work.'

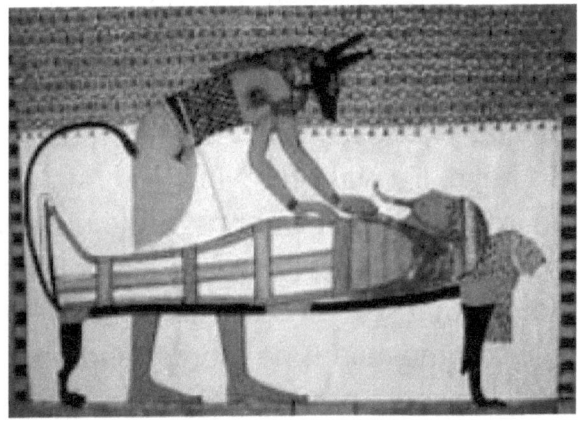

"The one shown in the picture entitled 'Picture showing my dad's embalmer at work, the picture shows a very fancy bed in its construction, as well as in its decoration. I looked at that one and determined that was where my dad was.

"One particularity about this process was that all embalmers were dressed in a particular way. They had a wrap around their waist and  a head set with the set being the head of Anubis. Naturally, the wrap and the head set were different, depending on whose body they were working on. The higher the grade of the priests, the fancier their clothing was.

"I immediately recognized my dad's gurney as it was the fanciest, and the priest that was working on my dad's body had the fanciest wrap and head set of the god Anubis. This is shown in the contrast between the two pictures that are shown here.

"My dad's body was laid out on the fancy table and was obviously already washed. His embalmer was working on his head. He was removing his brain via the nostrils with an iron hook, and what he could not reach with the hook was washed out with drugs. I kept watching what he was doing. That was all that was done for that day. The grand priest removed his headdress and proceeded to wash up and use some products on his body that I could not identify.

"The next day, my dear Kendall, I was there waiting for the grand priest to come and continue to mummify my dad. Soon after, he came to the premises with a bunch of priests. They were talking and joking about their work with the bodies of the dead people.

"Honestly, I did not like that. Anyway, once inside the building, the grand priest in charge of my dad's body proceeded to get ready for what was to come. He rubbed his body with some aromatic substance, then he took the headdress representing Anubis and put it over his head and said some prayers. He again opened my dad's flank and again cleaned and washed my dad's abdomen with palm wine and again with an infusion of ground spices. He then thoroughly rubbed the abdominal cavity with palm wine and with an infusion of ground spices. After that, he filled it with pure myrrh, cassia, and several other aromatic substances, excepting frankincense, and he sewed up my dad's flank again."

"Do you really have to tell me all the details, Khouf?"

"Yes, Kendall, as this is a famous process. Once this was done, my dad's body was removed from his gurney and was placed in some sort of large bathtub containing natron. They covered his body entirely with the natron. I learned from the conversation that was taking place that Dad's body would be left there for a period of seventy days.

"Let me tell you here that natron, known then as *Netjry*, the divine salt, was the key ingredient used in the mummification. Natron is a mixture of sodium bicarbonate, sodium carbonate, sodium sulphate, and sodium chloride that occurs naturally in many places in Egypt. A place where natron was found in quantities was in the Wadi Natrun. This place, my dear Kendal, is about sixty-four kilometers northwest of Cairo. The natron from this area has exceptional desiccating and defatting properties and was the preferred desiccant. Therefore, it was used for my dad's body.

"During these seventy days, so much occurred in my country. Rather than interrupt the entire process of my dad's embalmment and funeral, I will get back to these events once I tell you about how my dad was being prepared for the eternity."

"OK."

"At the end of the seventy days, the body of Dad was ready for the next step. At this time, his body was washed and then wrapped from head to foot in linen. This linen was cut into strips and smeared on the underside of his body with gum. Gum was commonly used then instead of glue.

"The priests and the embalmers had already advised

my mom that my dad's body was ready to be given to his family. My mom, helped by her sister, General Vas Nu Pieds, and Nanouka, had a wooden case made, shaped like a human figure, into which my dad's body would be put.

"Once my dad's body was put in the coffin, it was given back to my mom. She was there to receive the body where my dad's sister, who is General Vas Nu Pieds's wife, was also there. Old Man River and a few real close friends of my dad were there.

"My dad's Syrian wife and her son, now the heir to the throne of Egypt, as well as Twistmind, refused to join the family for my dad's funeral. They were busy plotting other activities. Normally, the heir to the throne of Egypt would be the person heading the family funerals. Since he refused to participate, it was my mom, General Vas Nu Pieds, and Nanouka who would head my dad's funeral. They would share this responsibility with the grand priest of the Karnack temple and the priests of my dad's palace. General Vas Nu Pieds also decided that my dad would have a military funeral reserved for the national heroes of Egypt. But that would have to wait for the moment.

"Every pharaoh, when enthroned, select's a site for his tomb, and the work starts in building the tomb almost imme-

PICTURE OF "KITES OF NEPHTHYS

diately. My dad, despite his young age, was no different from the other pharaohs. He chose a lot in the Valley of the Kings, and the carving of his tomb was almost completed at the moment of his death. What remains to be done was the painting of the different rooms of the tomb

This picture shows the kind of painting that is in a pharaoh's tomb.

and the usual furnishing that in the divine salt, the natron, the work in the normally goes with the entombing of the pharaoh.

In the seventy days during which my dad's body was plunged, the building of the tomb was accelerated, and I

was indirectly supervising its progress. It was so strange to see the devotion of the craftsmen painting the walls and ceilings of the tomb. They worked hard, and the painting of the walls and ceilings was completed before the seventy days. The workmen then furnished the tomb and provided it with all kinds of food and goodies. Then the work at the tomb was completed, and the premises was inspected by the grand priest and by General Vas Nus Pieds.

When they approved of the tomb's condition, the family and friends were ready for the funerals.

"My father's casket, my dear Kendall, was carried from the location of the embalmers to a location close to the grave site by priests of the higher rank. And it was placed on a special gurney where the family members could surround him.

"The funeral was a public affair at which, if one could

TOMB OF A PHARAOH WITH DIFFERENT CONTAINERS FOR FOOD AND OTHER ITEMS HE MAY NEED IN HIS ETERNAL LIFE

afford them, women were hired as professional mourners. These women were known as the Kites of Nephthys and would encourage people to express their grief through their own cries and lamentation. They would reference the brevity of life and how death came suddenly, but they would also give assurance of the eternal aspect of the soul and the confidence that the deceased would pass through the trial of the weighing of the heart in the after-

WHAT A PHARAOH TOMB LOOK LIKE WITH WALL DESIGNS

life by Osiris to pass on to paradise in the Field of Reeds.

"A lot of the grave's goods were placed in my dad's tomb. This was the custom regardless of the fact that the person that would be entered there was rich or poor. These would include shabti dolls who, in the afterlife, could be woken to life through a spell and assume the dead person's tasks.

Since the afterlife was

IIS IS WHAT A SHABTY BOX LOOKS LIKE

considered an eternal and perfect version of life on earth, it was thought there was work there just as in one's mortal life. The shabti would perform these tasks so the soul could relax and enjoy itself. At the time, the shabti dolls were important indicators to modern archaeologists on the wealth and status of the individual buried in a certain tomb. The more shabti dolls in a tomb, the wealthier the buried person was.

"Besides the shabti, my dad would be buried with items thought necessary in the afterlife: combs, jewelry, beer, bread, clothing, one's weapons, a favorite object, and even one's pets. All of these would appear to the soul in the afterlife, and they would be able to make use of them. Before the tomb was sealed, a ritual was enacted. It was considered vital to the continuation of the soul's journey—the Opening of the Mouth Ceremony. In this rite, a priest would invoke Isis and Nephthys (who had brought Osiris back to life) as he touches the mummy with different objects (adzes, chisels, knives) at various spots while anointing the body. In doing so, he would restore the use of ears, eyes, mouth, and nose to the deceased.

"The son and heir of the departed would often take the priest's role, thus further linking the rite with the story of Horus and his father Osiris. In my dad's situation, this did not take place because of what happened and how the heir of the throne of Egypt was selected.

"However, the grand priest invited General Vas Nus Pieds to take the priest's role, thus further linking the rite with the story of Horus and his father, Osiris.

Therefore, Vas Nus Pieds took care of the role which was considered vital for the continuation of the journey of my father's soul—the Opening of the Mouth Ceremony. My dad would now be able to hear, see, and speak and was ready to continue the journey. My dad's mummy would be enclosed in the sarcophagus, which would be buried in his grave, along with the grave goods, and the funeral would conclude. The living would then go back to their business, and the dead were then believed to go on to eternal life."

11 New Ruler, New Rules, and New Mess in Egypt

"So what happened to Egypt just after the gods ruled that my half-brother has become the heir to the throne of Egypt? Twistmind was named tutor of my half-brother, and quite a few things happened.

"General Vas Nus Pieds immediately started to investigate the murder of my father. He sent spies to all the countries on the east of Egypt. Obviously, the king of Syria, the father-in-law of the pharaoh, was also a recipient of one of these spies. This king was the one that received gifts from the pharaoh, and in return he sent back two urns with the heads of the ambassadors and the poisonous snakes, one of which bit and killed the pharaoh.

"At the same time, anticipating that his armed forces should be ready to respond to the country responsible to the killing of the pharaoh in such a cowardly and wicked manner, he undertook an intense training of all the Egyptian Armed Forces.

"The Egyptian army corps was organized into twenty companies. Each company had between two hundred and two hundred fifty soldiers. The Egyptian military was a firm organization of professional soldiers. Many who served in the Egyptian army were described as mercenaries, but they were most likely prisoners who preferred the life of a soldier to that of slavery.

"The Egyptians' chariots were lighter and faster than those of other major powers in the Middle East. Egyptian war chariots were manned by drivers holding whips and reins and by fighters wielding composite bows. After spending all his arrows, a fighter would use a short spear, of which he had a few.

"The principal weapon of the Egyptian army was the bow and arrow, which became a formidable weapon with the introduction of the composite bow. These bows, combined with the war chariot, enabled the Egyptian army to attack quickly and from a distance. Another weapon that the Egyptian army used was the khopesh. The khopesh is a bronze sword with a short handle that ends with a sharp curve.

"The general also arranged the embalmment and funeral of the pharaoh. He consoled and cared for his wife, the pharaoh's sister, as well as for the pharaoh's wife. In order to arrange for the pharaoh's funeral, there were two sets of activities that had to be completed. These were the embalmment of the pharaoh and making the tomb of the pharaoh ready to receive his body. In this situation, the body was ready, but the tomb needed two to three months for the completion of the construction work and of the necessary furnishing and decoration in accordance with our traditions. Considering these factors, after consulting with the widow and others as required, he decided that the pharaoh's funeral should not take place sooner than five months from then, so he set the date accordingly.

"The first thing Twistmind did was to act in such a way as to be clearly shown as the lover of the Syrian widow of the dead pharaoh. The other thing that Twistmind did was that he managed to become the tutor of my half-brother. After being named tutor, he took over and decided all by himself how and when the crowning of my half-brother should be.

"Abiding by the traditions, he set a date for the crowning exactly one month after the pharaoh's funerals. He wanted this event to be a very international affair, so he invited not only the Egyptian officials that normally attended such events but also several rulers and kings from the countries around Egypt. Among the rulers and kings invited was the king of Syria, who had sent the two urns with the ambassador's heads and the snakes that killed the pharaoh.

"As soon as that was known in the country, a real conflict took place between the armed forces and my half-brother's entourage. Twistmind used all kinds of sorcery and tricks to overrule the armed forces and General Vas Nu Pieds. The general was furious, and so were my mother, my family, and our friends, as well as many other people. That became an incentive for General Vas Nu Pieds. Soon the spies that the general had sent to Syria returned, and the news that they brought were not good. The king of Syria was planning to come for the crowning of his grandchild, bringing with him an entourage of politicians and a small army 'just in case.'

"Everyone in Syria also apparently knew what happened to the bodies of the two ambassadors whose heads were in the urns. This was because they were executed publicly. They also knew that the two were decapitated and that their heads were to be sent back to the pharaoh. Everyone also knew what happened to their bodies. They were given to the dogs to eaten in the same public place where they were executed. That was done for the Syrian people to know what the king thought about the pharaoh of Egypt. Can you believe that?

"This reinforced the need that Vas Nu Pieds felt and prepared for. That was also the time when he was told that the tomb of the pharaoh was ready and fully furnished and that the food required was in place. This food was in the pharaoh's tomb for him to eat when in the other world. So my mom and Vas Nu Pieds decided on the date of the funeral, and they also decided to make it private, telling only those who should know. So it was done. My half-brother and his mom, as well as other officials, were told the day before the event. And thank god they declined to come. So the pharaoh was buried without the presence of the usurper.

"Immediately after Vas Nu Pieds returned to his military barracks, he prepared to leave with his army to encounter the king of Syria. He knew from the spy that the king was coming with a small army to enter as a victor in Memphis, then in Thebes.

"Without the knowledge of Vas Nus Pieds, I jumped on the back of his chariot and comfortably sat there. Yes, my dear Kendall, I was there, ready to watch the show. That allowed me to see and to describe all that was happening without being seen.

"Vas Nus Pieds decided that he would wait for the king of Syria at the frontiers of Egypt. He planned to hide about the three-quarters of his army and would wait for the king with about a quarter of his troops to make it look like a very small—maybe a welcoming—committee. About a week later, he moved to the frontier and waited, as if he were there to welcome the king. Soon two Syrian soldiers riding horses appeared. The general was very courteous with them and told them he was waiting for the Syrian king to welcome him his way. They did not get the meaning of this sentence and returned to the king, telling him that an escort was waiting for him.

"Soon the king appeared. As he got closer, the general,

followed by a few of his 'guard-de-corps,' went to the king. When he was close enough, he asked him if he was the king of Syria. The king responded yes, so the general loudly told him that he was not welcome in Egypt and that he better return to his country. The king responded that he was the guest of the heir of the throne of Egypt and of his tutor, as well as of his own daughter, who was the widow of the dead pharaoh. General Vas Nu Pieds again told him that he was not welcome in Egypt. 'By which authority?' asked the king. 'By mine,' responded the general.

"'So you still want to come?' asked the general. The king gave orders to the small army that was accompanying him to attack the general with his small group of officers. So they did.

"I was there, Kendall. No one paid attention to a small and insignificant frog. I witnessed the entire show, being secured behind a large stone. As soon as the Syrian soldiers reached the small group of Egyptian officers, the rest of the soldiers that were hiding counterattacked.

"In the melee, the Syrian army did not realize that the Egyptian Armed Forces, divided into two groups, attacked them from the two sides, encircling them with the general and his small group facing them. The Syrians were no match for this army and were being massacred. With nowhere to go, the king realized that he had no chance to win, and he wanted to retreat and go back home.

He could not do so, as he was encircled. He then advanced alone to talk to the Egyptian general. For a moment, the battle stopped between the general's small group of soldiers and the king's forces.

"'What is it?' asked the general.

"'I want to retreat and go back home to Syria.'

"'Too late,' responded Vas Nu Pieds. 'Did you kill the ambassadors of peace sent to you by the pharaoh? Did you send their heads in two urns with all the snakes inside them, including the snake that killed the pharaoh? Did you feed the bodies of the two Egyptian ambassadors to the dogs in a public place in your capital, Your Majesty?'

"'Uh.'

"'Then there is a price to pay to come to my beloved country. So come and fight as a man, sire. I will fight you alone. So for a moment, the fight will be between you and me.'

"So the two took positions in their chariots and started to fight. It did not take long for Vas Nu Pieds to push the driver of the king's chariot out with his spear and down the chariot, leaving the Syrian king alone and incapable to fight and drive. Being in this situation, he threw his khopesh and raised his two arms to surrender. Vas Nu Pieds ordered two of his soldiers to go and take the king from his chariot and bring him to him. He also took the king's khopesh."

"What is a khopesh, Khouf?"

"A khopesh is a short bronze sword that ends with a sharp curve and has a short handle, Kendall.

"General Vas Nu Pieds kept the king's khopesh as a souvenir, with a planned use for it that no one knew.

"The king was brought to the general held by the two Egyptian soldiers, each soldier holding the king's arms.

"'I will spare your life and let the Egyptian people decide what to do to you. I will take you to Egypt and tie your two arms to a beam held on your back and have my soldiers hold the two sides of the beam. You will also walk barefoot,' said General Vas Nu Pieds.

"What the general said was then done. The rest of the

king's army had every soldier hold their hands over their heads. They walked barefoot behind their king, framed by the Egyptian soldiers.

"Vas Nu Pieds turned around and started returning to Egypt toward the city of Memphis. Soon close to the frontier, the general and his army found themselves facing my half-brother, Syroman, the pharaoh-to-be, with a very small group of his palace guards.

"The general asked him, 'Where are you going, Syroman?'

"Syroman answered, 'I am going to receive my grandfather, the king of Syria. I invited him to my crowning as pharaoh.'

"'You invited the murderer of your father to your crowning?' said the general.

"'He is my grandfather,' responded Syroman.

"'Do you know what a traitor is, Syroman? You are a traitor to your country as well as to your family. Soldiers, arrest him and let him join his grandfather. Egypt can do without people like you.'

"'But I am the pharaoh-to-be. You cannot do that. I order you not to do that.'

"'Well, keep your orders to yourself. And yes, I can do that, and I am doing it. Soldiers, arrest him and tie him next to his grandfather. And take his shoes off.'

"'No, no, you cannot do that. I order you not to do that.'

"'Soldiers, arrest him and tie him next to his grandfather. And take his shoes off. There is enough space for the two of you along this beam.'

"Then, addressing the small group of Syroman's guards, he said, 'Soldiers, you can dismantle and you can either join my soldiers or you can go back home.'

"It took General Vas Nu Pieds and his soldiers and prisoners a day and half to reach the city of Memphis as they were walking slowly because of his prisoners.

"Just before they entered the city, one of the Syrian king's prisoners ran away from where he was located at the first row of the king's prisoners toward the chariot of General Vas Nu Pieds, stealing on his way a spear from an Egyptian soldier to attempt to harm or kill Vas Nu Pieds. Hearing the commotion and seeing the soldier advancing toward him, he took his archer and, faster than the arrow, he was holding killed this solder.

"He then instructed one of the soldiers in the first row behind him as follows: 'Soldier, move the corpse of this dead soldier out of our way, right there in the middle of the desert, so that any wild animal will eat this corpse.'

"He then turned to address the king's soldiers that were prisoners. He told them with a very high voice, 'Soldiers, probably by tomorrow, all that will remain of this soldier's corpse will be his bones.'

"He ended his talk, telling them, 'Any one of you will be welcome to be killed and join this soldier.'"

Then Khouf addressed himself to Kendall and said, "Kendall, I am giving you this story in detail so you will know that your country of origin does not allow itself to be ruled by traitors. You can be proud to be a blood princess of Egypt. One day, I hope you will travel there and see with your eyes the great country of your ancestors.

"Now back to my description of what happened. Soon Vas Nu Pieds and his suite were at the edge of the city of Memphis. There, the general asked that his troops refresh themselves. Then he chose five men, four of which were his more articulate soldiers, and asked them to go to Memphis to make the following announcement:

"'Good people of Memphis, listen to this important announcement. General Vas Nu Pieds is returning from his battle against the king of Syria and has the king himself, as well as the small army that was with him, as his prisoners.'

"'Also tell them this in a separate announcement for more impact: "Good people of Memphis, listen to this other important announcement. General Vas Nu Pieds also arrested Prince Syroman as a traitor to Egypt for inviting the murderer of his father as a guest to his coronation as pharaoh and for going himself to receive him with all the honors due to a chief of state. You should know that by doing so, he saved Egypt, his beloved country, from the subjugation to the king of Syria."'

"He gave his soldiers a day to announce him and his forces to the city of Memphis. He took that day for him and his soldiers to refresh themselves. The fifth man sent to Memphis was to find and buy a cage made of wood that could be put on top of a carriage. This cage should be such as its four vertical walls be made of bamboo spaced such that whoever was inside this cage could be viewed. And it should be solid enough not to allow anyone to escape. It did not matter if the cage was new or already existed and used before.

"During this day, the general and his troops relaxed and enjoyed their victory.

"My dear Kendall, what happed the next morning, late in the morning, the general decided that this was a good time to enter the city at the head of his troops. And with his soldiers and prisoners following him, he entered the city.

"What he did not expect was that the city streets were filled with people on the two side of the road, shouting and welcoming him as a conqueror. And many were greeting him as the new pharaoh. He tried to appease the crowd's enthusiasm and excitement to no avail. People shouted their welcome, and many started to shout, 'Your Majesty, Vas Nu Pieds, may you live, prosper, and be healthy!' That was the way of addressing the pharaoh.

"Kendall, my beautiful princess, you would not believe the size and the happiness of the crowd in addressing the general and his troops. He crossed the city and went directly to the army caserns in Memphis where his troops were very tired and were ready to relax.

"There he also found the cage exactly as he wanted. He had his two prisoners transferred to the cage and tied up to the vertical bamboo in such a way as to let them be able to sleep. Despite the fact that normally prisoners were not given any importance to their comfort, Vas Nu Pieds decided to do so, as he understood the humanity of all men even if they were his prisoners.

"When his troops went to relax and sleep, the general ordered to have fifty horses ready for the next day's travel to Thebes. It was then after knowing that he was going to have his horses ready for the next day and deciding with his assistant soldiers who would be the soldiers that would use these horses that he also asked that the horses be on the side of Memphis that is on the road toward Thebes. Then he decided to relax and have some sleep.

"The next day, a little before noon, the general put his troops in formation and finally entered the city. The city went wild. People were alongside the road, and they were shouting and saying, 'Thank you, thank you, my general. May you live, prosper, and be healthy.' They addressed him like he was a pharaoh. He honestly did not expect this, as he was a humble man from the people despite the fact that he married the sister of the pharaoh.

"One of his soldiers, with a loud and clear voice, using an instrument that looked like a large cone with the short end trunked, was shouting again and again with his mouth inside the cone: 'Good people of Egypt, listen to this important announcement. General Vas Nu Pieds is returning from his battle against the king of Syria and has the king himself, as well as the small army that was with him, as his prisoners.'

Also tell them in a separate announcement for more impact:

"'Good people of Egypt, listen to this other important announcement. General Vas Nu Pieds also arrested Prince Syroman as a traitor to Egypt for inviting the murderer of his father as a guest to his coronation as pharaoh and for going himself to receive him with all the honors due to a chief of state. You should know that by doing so, General Vas Nu Pieds saved Egypt, his beloved country, and all of the people of Egypt from the subjugation to the king of Syria.'

"He also let the people know for the first time that this king also murdered the two ambassadors sent to him by the pharaoh with gifts as a gesture of peace and friendship, as one of his wives was the daughter of this king. He further had the two ambassadors' heads placed in the urns that he sent to the pharaoh with serpents, with the intention that one of the serpents would bite and kill the pharaoh. The soldier with the loud voice also told the crowd that this king gave the bodies of the ambassadors to be eaten by his dogs.

"The soldier with the loud voice and with a trunked device also told the people that the second man in the cage was Syroman, the other son of the pharaoh—the young man who was supposed to become the next pharaoh. This man was a traitor that invited the king of Syria to his crowning, knowing that the king was the murderer of his father, he and his mother, Merdocine, as well as her lover, the sorcerer Twistmind, who was also the tutor of Syroman, jointly invited the king of Syria. So the three of them were accomplices and traitors in this invitation. The general assures you all, the people of Egypt, that the mother and tutor will be arrested as soon as he enters Thebes and will hand them to the priests of the temple of Karnack.

"The people were shouting, '"Death to the king of Syria, death to the traitors, death to the cruel murderer, and death to the traitors.'

"When the general and his troops arrived at the other side of Memphis, my dear Kendall, he found the fifty horses waiting for him and his troops. The members of his troops he chose to use the fifty horses moved to their selected horses. The rest of his troops would travel to Thebes by other means of transportation. They would not become part of the triumphal entry of General Vas Nu

Pieds.

"So the general, followed by his prisoners in their cage and by his troops, left Memphis toward Thebes. There were several cities and villages between Memphis and Thebes, and every time he entered a city or a village, he was received as a hero and a conqueror. Before entering a city or a village, the soldier with the loud voice would go ahead of the general and his troops. He would shout and tell the people of every village and city about the two people that were in the cage. They were the king of Syria, who was the murderer of the pharaoh, and Syroman, the other son of the pharaoh and the young man who was supposed to become the next pharaoh. He added that Syroman was arrested because he was a traitor that invited the king of Syria, the murderer of his father, to his crowning.

"The soldier with the loud voice did not have to introduce the general as the people recognized him and cheered him and his troops. But the people were shouting, 'Death to the king, death to the traitors, death to the cruel murderer, and death to the traitors.'

"After two days of traveling through cities and villages, the general and his troops finally arrived in Thebes. Before entering the city of Thebes, the soldier with the loud voice would again go ahead of the general and his troops. He would shout and tell the people of Thebes that the two people that were in the cage were the king of Syria, who was the murderer of the pharaoh, and Syroman, the other son of the pharaoh and who was the young man who was supposed to become the next pharaoh. The general and his troops and prisoners were received with people lining up on the two sides of the streets, shouting,

'Our general, may you live, prosper, and be healthy. You should be our pharaoh. You should be our pharaoh.' They kept repeating this phrase, first timidly, then more boldly until it became a refrain that all the people kept shouting. Every street he went in with his troops, people were shouting the same refrain. The general tried to calm the crowd as much as he could and he kept going toward the palace of the pharaoh. Once there, he immediately went to the quarters of the pharaoh's wives, and the first person that came out of these quarters was Twistmind.

"The general, in his parade uniform and riding his horse, faced Twistmind and told him, 'Twistmind, you are under arrest for treason.'

"He then instructed two of his soldiers to come down from their horses and take Twistmind and throw him into the cage with the two other prisoners. Twistmind did not have time to react or use his tricks as a sorcerer before finding himself in the cage with the king of Syria and his pupil.

"Then the general shouted loudly the name of Merdocine. After doing this a couple of times, she came out barefoot and dressed in her house dress, and found herself herself face-to-face with the general's horse. She looked up to see who was calling her. Again the general addressed her. He told her, 'Merdocine, you are under arrest for treason.'

"Then he instructed two of his soldiers to take her and throw her into the cage with the three other prisoners. Merdocine and Twistmind hardly realized what was happening to them when Vas Nu Pieds told them, 'The four of you are to be taken to the grand priest of Karnack to be judged. The king of Syria will be judged for the murder of

the pharaoh, and Merdocine, her son, and her lover will
be judged for high treason against Egypt.'

12 The Making of a Pharaoh

"The general then left the palace and directed himself toward Karnack via the long way crossing the city of Thebes. Naturally, he again directed the soldier with the loud voice to go ahead of the general and his troops and to shout to the people of Thebes that the four people that were in the cage were the king of Syria, Syroman, Merdocine, and her lover, the sorcerer Twistmind. These three were guilty of treason to the country.

"Now, my dear Kendall, that the three people responsible for treason—Syroman, his mother, and Twistmind—were under arrest, they would not be able to harm this country again.

"The soldier with the loud voice kept repeating the same thing again and again. Naturally, this attracted lots of people alongside of the roads, and the crowd started to shout very loudly, 'Our general, may you live, prosper, and be healthy. You should be our pharaoh. You should be our pharaoh. Long life to our new pharaoh, the savior of our beloved Egypt.'

"They kept repeating this phrase, first timidly, then it became a refrain that all people kept shouting. Every street he went in with his troops, people were shouting the same. The general tried to calm the crowd as much as he could, as he kept going toward the temple of Karnack. After a good moment, he stopped and asked two soldiers by name to come and talk to him. He instructed them to run at great speed to the temple and let the grand priest know that he was coming with his prisoners to give them to him for their trials. He also asked them to tell the priests there how and what happened that led to their victory.

"As the procession of the general and his troops and prisoners kept advancing in Thebes, the crowds got more exited and started to throw stones at the prisoners in the cage.

"The general shouted, 'No, don't throw stones. Please don't throw stones.' But the people continued to show their rage for the assassination of the pharaoh. To avoid the prisoners being lynched, the general started to advance faster for parading the prisoners to the crowds.

"'Our general, may you live, prosper, and be healthy. You should be our pharaoh. You should be our pharaoh.'

They kept repeating this phrase, first timidly then it became a refrain that all people kept shouting. Every street he went in with his troops, people were shouting the same. The general tried to calm the crowd as much as he could, and kept going soon they arrived at the temple.

The convoy had not have enough time to put itself together in the right formation to enter the temple, when the sound of music and singing of the priests was heard by all of those who were with the general. Wow, what a reception the general and his soldiers had by the priests of the temple of Karnack. Priests were lining the entrance of the temple on the two sides and were playing their instruments as well as singing. The words of their songs were 'our general, may you live, prosper, and be healthy. Our general, you should be our pharaoh. You should be our pharaoh.'

"They kept repeating this phrase again and again as the convoy was going through the temple to meet with the grand priest. Soon they arrived there. The grand priest, and also all the priests in the temple, had already heard of the general's battle with the king of Syria. They also heard that the general arrested Syroman, his mother, and Twistmind and kept them as prisoners on grounds of treason.

"This would explain, my dear Kendall, the reception that they received at the temple.

"The grand priest and the reception committee composed of other priests and of important members of the temple organization, as well as of dignitaries of the late pharaoh, were  all there, waiting for the general and his forces, as well as for the prisoners. As soon as the general faced the grand priest, he went down his horse and bent himself all the way down as a form of respect to the grand priest.

Immediately, the grand priest stood up and went to him and invited him to stand up. He hugged the general and invited him to sit down next to him. "The general was now standing up, and he greeted the grand priest by telling him, 'Your Most Venerable Priest, may you live a long life, prosper, and be healthy. I am bringing to you these prisoners for you to judge and punish according to the laws of Egypt. And if these four people are found guilty with the people as witness of their punishment, instruct me where would you like me to take them, and I will put them there.'

"The grand priest then instructed a group of priests and a group of guards to advance. And he told the general that these men will take charge of them. The general then instructed a group of his soldiers to help carry the cage and to hand it to the guards, which they did.

"The grand priest then addressed the general and said, 'Thank you. Thank you, General Vas Nu Pieds. You saved our country. You saved us all from the humiliation of being controlled by Syria and by its murderer king that killed our pharaoh. Thank you. Thank you, General Vas Nu Pieds. You saved our country. You saved us all from the humiliation of being ruled by a traitor to our beloved country.'

"He then added, 'We the priests of the Karnack temple will take care of these criminals according to our country's laws. For the moment, Egypt is without a ruler, but that should not be. Therefore, the council of the priests of the temple of Karnack has decided that the only person that can rule the country with love and respect is the one that saved the country from being humiliated from a ruler who is a traitor or from a foreign king.

This person is you, General Vas Nu Pieds. Please accept this responsibility as well as this honor.'

"'Oh god, Amun-Ra! It would indeed be a great honor for a humble person of the people who became a soldier of this great country and then was promoted to become a general and was allowed to marry the sister of our pharaoh. Yes, it is a great honor for me. And under the present circumstances, if it is the will of the highest moral and religious authority of my beloved Egypt to take over the ruling of this country, I would humbly accept this responsibility if I would have the blessing of the god Amun-Ra.'

"The grand priest then said, 'The god Amun-Ra was consulted as you were coming here, and you have his blessing and his best wishes. He said that you shall be a great pharaoh, should you accept this responsibility.'

"Vas Nu Pieds then answered, 'I do accept this honor and responsibility, Grand Priest, and I will often ask your advice as I rule this great country.'

"The grand priest then solemnly said, 'I therefore, by the authority bestowed upon me by the council of the Karnack temple and as the Hemu of the Pr-Ntr-Kmt, do appoint you as Egypt's pharaoh. Your Majesty, may you live a long life, prosper, and be healthy. Please choose the name with which you will govern this wonderful country.'

"'I am choosing the name Ramses XXIII to rule Egypt, and I swear that I will rule this country fairly, with wisdom, love, and to the best I can. I will request your help and wisdom to better the life of all Egyptians and to keep its glorious history always alive and glittering among all nations.'

"That was the response of Vas Nu Pieds, my dear Kendall, and that brought a change of dynasty for Egypt.

"The grand priest then asked the priests next to him to bring the clothes that a pharaoh normally wears, which had been prepared in advance for the general. And when they were brought in, the grand priest helped Vas Nu Pieds put them on. Then the grand priest bowed all the way down to the floor and addressed the new pharaoh as follows:

"'Your Majesty, Pharaoh Ramses XXIII, may you live a

long life, prosper, and be healthy. Please ride your horse. I will do the same and join you in crossing the city to your new palace. That will be the way for you to be introduced to the people of Thebes as the new pharaoh. We shall have the soldier with the loud voice introduce you to the crowd and repeat again and again, "Bow to your new pharaoh. Bow to His Majesty, Pharaoh Ramses XXIII. May he live a long life, prosper, and be healthy.'

"What was said was done. A priest brought a horse for the grand priest and helped him ride it. Then the procession started, and the soldier with the loud voice introduced the pharaoh to the crowd. Naturally, this attracted lots of people alongside of the roads, and the crowd bowed all the way to the ground and started to shout very loudly again and again, "Your Majesty, Pharaoh Ramses XXIII, may you live a long life, prosper, and be healthy." They showed their joy, and the crowd was a jolly mess of shouting and singing.

"The convoy stopped first in the general's home to take his wife, Nanouka. It was a great surprise to her, to Old Man River, and to her house servants when they found out what happened. All of them started to shout 'Hallelujah, halleluiah.' They kept shouting loudly,

"'Our pharaoh, may you live a long life, prosper, and be healthy. Vas Nu Pieds kissed his wife, then the two of them jumped in a carriage, and the grand priest joined them in another carriage. The entire convoy with the pharaoh, grand priest, and the soldiers proceeded to go to the palace to meet the widow of the deceased predecessor.

"On the way to the palace, although no soldier was introducing the new pharaoh, the crowd, now informed by word of mouth, kept welcoming the new pharaoh. They yelled hallelujah and kept shouting again and again, 'Your Majesty, Pharaoh Ramses XXIII, may you live a long life, prosper, and be healthy. Halleluiah.'

"As they were showing their joy, the crowd was a jolly mess. The crowd was shouting and singing their joy for the new pharaoh. Soon the convoy arrived at the palace.

It was received with joy and deference.

All who were there went out to receive the convoy. The pygmy Deneg started to dance and do acrobatics. The women of the two harems, their children, the blood princesses, and the foreign princesses left their respective areas and welcomed the new pharaoh with dancing and singing for him. Nanouka, the wife of the deceased pharaoh, came to him and greeted him as the new pharaoh by bowing all the way to the floor and saying the same thing everyone was saying: 'Your Majesty, Pharaoh Ramses XXIII, may you live a long life, prosper, and be healthy. Halleluiah.'

"He and his wife immediately left his chariot and went to her. They hugged her and kissed her and promised to give her dead husband another funeral—this time the one of a glorious pharaoh killed. Then the pharaoh turned toward the two young adolescents that also came to welcome him and said, 'My two friends, Mange Ta Soupe and Jon-Jon Tee, as of now you are under my protection. The traitor Syroman will bother you no more. Mange Ta Soupe, I know that he tried to rape you and wanted to kill you for not accepting his advances. I also know that Jon-Jon saved you by making you look like an old witch. As for you, Jon-Jon, continue to protect your friend Mange Ta Soupe. You shall be rewarded, and I know that Khouf's Ka is and shall always be with you.' Then he added, 'I shall be ruling the country as of now out of my house, and I will not move to the pharaoh's suite yet in the palace. I want Nanouka to remain there until a new suite is built for her near the pharaoh's suite in the palace. I will also build a monument to commemorate the life of the murdered pharaoh, as well as the short life of Khouf, who was killed in order to give Syroman, the traitor, the throne of Egypt. This monument shall be in the palace between the two suites—the pharaoh's and the next suite that will be built for the widow of the last pharaoh.'

"He then asked the chamberlain who was there to assist him and to remain in his position as his chamberlain. And he asked him as his first task to take note and have his orders executed. With this said, he turned around, rode his carriage, and took his wife on the carriage with him. And the soldiers and the group that were part of his suite directed themselves back to his home.

"As of now, my dear Kendall, I stopped following him. I knew then that he would rule the country like my dad would and would bring to it a glorious future. He still had to name a new ruler for Syria, which became a country occupied by Egypt, and it remained a vassal to it.

"As you remember, I left, assured that Egypt was in good hands. I went north, still looking for this Egyptian princess that would kiss me at the right time. My condition as a frog allowed me to be almost invisible. When I was in the port of what is now Alexandria, I was investigating a large container when it was put on the boat. There I stayed until it was unloaded in a port in Europe. When they opened this container, I left it and began to wander in this new country. How different things were there. People were dressed differently and spoke a language I could not understand. I stayed there for some time and really did not like it.

"Again I found a boat that I thought was returning to Egypt, and I was there for a very long time. I did not know where the boat was going. Was it weeks or months? I don't know, Kendall. Then finally, the boat arrived at a port. There I found other kinds of people. Some were dressed like those in European ports, and others were dressed in strange clothing. They had feathers over their heads and spoke a different language from those that were dressed like Europeans. After some time, I realized I was in what is today the United States of America.

"I wandered there, attempting to learn their language. First I did not know which language to learn. Should I learn the language of the feathered people or the language of the people dressed like Europeans? Although there were more feathered people than those in European dress, the European-dressed people seemed to be in control as they had killing instruments and were not shy to use them against the feathered ones. Not playing politics in my condition, I decided to learn the European people's language. It took me a very long time to do so, but I finally got there. After that, I started to investigate and look for the Egyptian princess that would help me regain my life. It took me a long time, but I found you, my princess. And that was it."

13 What Now?

The moral of this story is that crime certainly does not pay. Often the price of such acts is going to jail for a long time or death. If such consequences do not occur right away, the criminals would still not enjoy the product of their crime as they would always be on the lookout for the police trying to catch them. And their consciences will bother them about the crime. I needed to share this last thought with you, and now I did.

"Now, my dear Kendall, is the moment of truth. You saved me, and you very attentively listened to me all this time. Let this be the way I want to pay my debt back."

"Pay me back for what?"

"Before disappearing from your life, there are a few secrets that are not yet discovered that I will give you, and that could make you famous and celebrated all over the world if you use them. First I invite you to visit the country of your ancestors, where you are a real princess by birth. This will hopefully induce you to be interested in Egyptology. And if so, it may also induce you to become an Egyptologist."

"You want me to become an Egyptologist? Is that what you want me to do?"

"Want you, no. Wish that you do, yes. Should this happen, then the secrets that I am about to tell you will help you become very famous in this world. This will happen because for decades, the Egyptologists from all around the world are trying to discover these secrets."

"And these are?"

"First I will tell you about the three pyramids of Giza—the Cheops, the Khafre, and the Menkaure pyramids. These pyramids were built after the stepped pyramid

of Djoser in Sakkara, which was built after the mastaba tomb was built.

The mastaba tomb had a small palace built under it as an afterlife residence for the pharaoh that built it. Unfortunately, thieves discovered the pharaoh's tomb and stole all the precious things that they contained. The same happened to Sakkara's stepped pyramid. Well, that inspired three pharaohs—Cheops, Khafre, and Menkaure—to place their afterlife palaces in their pyramids in an area that would be impossible to be reached by the thieves looking to rob the tombs."

"And how did they do that?"

"To totally disrupt the thieves' plans, three chambers were built inside the Great Pyramid. The lowest chamber was cut into the bedrock upon which the pyramid was built and was unfinished. The queen's chamber and the king's chamber are higher up within the pyramid structure. The king's chamber contained an empty sarcophagus and was made easy to reach. That left the three pyramids' real palace tombs undisturbed by the thieves."

"Good. That was smart. So how do you think I will be smarter than those who designed these chambers or the thieves who, for so many generations, tried to rob these tombs?"

"Because I will tell you how. As a frog, I could be in places where I could hear architects, priests, and some builders talk about the secrets of the pyramids. The way for you to reach the palaces built in each of these pyramids is to build a small tunnel leading from above or below the king's chamber and toward the outside of the pyramid. As you do this, you should use first a new kind of x-ray that can penetrate the stone of the pyramid. That would indicate where the void is. It will be toward this void that you should dig this small tunnel.

"Somewhere along this tunnel, you will find a wall blocking the door of the pharaoh's death residence. I know it because I saw the plans used to build these pyramids. Wow, that discovery will make you famous all over the world. Naturally, it won't be easy to get the permission from the Egyptian authorities to dig such a tunnel. You would first have to secure the help of the Egyptian authorities and of a civil engineer to design such a tunnel to make sure that the pyramid will not collapse or eventually affect any palace under it."

"Yes, but I don't know if I will be up to that or if I would like to do something like that."

"You don't know that now, but here is a second discovery you could make if you become an Egyptologist. This would be the tomb of Alexander the Great of Greece. This tomb is located in the city center of Alexandria, somewhere south of the intersection of Al Horreya and el-Nebi Daniel Street. But this exact location has not been located and may in fact be beneath the mosque of Nebi Daniel or in a nearby Greek necropolis.

"The third discovery you could make if you become an Egyptologist is the tombs of the Ptolemaic pharaohs. There are thirteen of them. These tombs are believed to be located under the rails of the tramways connecting Alexandria city center and the area known as Ramleh. They are most probably between Alexandria Ramleh Station and the station named Ibrahimia along the railroad of the tramways.

"The fourth discovery you could make if you become an Egyptologist is the remnant of the palace of Cleopatra that is actually buried on the seashore of Alexandria. Some of that is already under study, but it seems that a large portion of the palace and of what surrounds it was taken by the sea during the year 365 tsunami.

"This tsunami was the result of a powerful earthquake off the coast of Greece, which was thought to have had a magnitude of 8.0. The Alexandria tsunami's wave rushed in and carried the Alexandria port ships over the sea walls, landing many on top of buildings. In Alexandria, approximately five thousand people lost their lives, and fifty thousand homes were destroyed. Among the buildings destroyed were lots of buildings of the old city, including Cleopatra's palace, and other Ptolemaic homes and palaces.

"These are, my dear, some of the discoveries you may make. Well, the time has come for me to bid farewell and go. All that I have been telling you would appear to you like dreams, and you shall not forget them. However, as I go, please remember that you owe to the country of which you are a princess to act like one, and you shall be remembered.

"When I go, please take my ashes and bury them in

a place that will remind you of me." With these words, Khouf, the prince of Egypt, started disappearing, and all that remained was some dust in the floor and some tears in Kendall's eyes.

About the Author

Fernand W. Dahan is an 85-year-old retired architect. He is an expert in the design of many types of laboratories. He has a bachelor's degree of architecture and master's degrees in city and regional planning, was awarded many awards for his work in his field, and is a fellow of the American Institute of Architects. Being a fellow is a high honor bestowed on very few architects for work that has made a significant contribution to architecture and society on a national level. He speaks English, French, Arabic and Spanish.

He was the author of *"Laboratories: A Guide to Planning, Programming, and Design,"* published by W.W. Norton. He also coauthored *"The Public Service Career Program Plan, Planning Guide,"* published by the Department of Labor in 1973, and many articles in the field of laboratories that were published in architecture and engineering publications. He was also the author of a theater play.

He has been a guest lecturer at Georgetown University and the American University in Cairo, Egypt, and he has lectured at several AIA national conventions, at a HVAC national convention, and at two international architectural conventions. You may Google the author for more information on him and his work.

www.ingramcontent.com/pod-product-compliance
Lightning Source LLC
Chambersburg PA
CBHW031948170626
46807CB00006B/2395